3 QUEENS
An Unforgettable Urban Romance
2

A NOVEL BY

PORSCHA STERLING

JOIN MY MAILING LIST!

Join my mailing list to stay up to date on my blog posts, news and my new releases. I also run many contests that are only mentioned to my mailing list subscribers.

Click this link to join or text PORSCHA to 25827

To submit a manuscript for my review, go here or go to www. royaltypublishinghouse.com and visit the 'Submissions' page.

ACKNOWLEDGMENTS

This book has been a long time coming!

I have to first thank God for giving me the ability and courage to follow my dreams. Plenty of days I have doubted myself, but He gave me the courage to pursue what I knew I could do.

I want to thank my muse, Karenina Simmons, for talking me through the lives of these complicated storylines only for me to change everything once I started to write; my "Momty", Nedra Bates, and my mother for being my first cheerleaders – always in my corner no matter what.

Last but never, EVER least, I want to thank my favorite two year old, **Alphonzo,** for allowing mommy the time to write – you are amazing and I do everything ALL for you!

SYNOPSIS

Jazymn has a big secret that she is keeping from her boyfriend, Kingston, and she vows never to tell him. She's happy in love and she was able to get rid of his wife, Shanice, so all should be well...or so she thought. When Kingston finds out the truth about what Jazmyn did to ensure her happily ever after, all hell breaks loose and she is left with more than a broken heart.

Kaylen has found new love after being abused and misused by the man she thought loved her. But everything with Caleb is not all peaches and cream. But it never is when you're dating a womanizer. After too many run-ins with one of Caleb's old groupies, Kaylen sheds off the business professional and brings out the ratchet to settle the matter with the side chick from hell. But, in the process, she finds out something that makes her think twice about whether what she has with Caleb is real. This discovery leads her back into the arms of Lorenzo, who is all too ready to lick her wounds and steal her heart.

After Alexis was assaulted by someone she trusted, she finds solace in a secret life that allows her to become the dominant one and inflict the pain she feels on others. Although her husband tries to love her, she rejects him at every turn. But Alexis isn't the only one with the secret life. Marc has one, too. Alexis may think she's the pampered wife of a corporate millionaire but in actuality, her husband is as street as they come.

ALEXIS

ick and suck. Lick and suck...rinse, repeat. Do the shit again. Alexis moaned on cue as John lapped at her breast while fumbling with his jeans. She pushed him off of her and finished tugging them off with ease before pushing him down onto the bed. She'd had enough practice to know what she was doing. Her movements were almost mechanical in nature. She had been taught well and she did as she was told. She sucked her teeth as she looked at him sitting on the bed wide-eyed like a deer in headlights.

"Lay down." She said with her signature tone of arrogance, confidence and power. John rushed to do as she asked. He dropped down backwards onto the bed with his belly in the air, exposing his 3-inch erection. Alexis tried hard to stifle the laugh that was beginning in her throat. She'd seen some small ones in the past few months, but this here was just ridiculous.

"I meant face down. Turn the fuck over." Alexis watched John scramble to flip over as she grabbed her equipment of torture. She adjusted the top of her leather vest and picked up the whip that she used for her first round. She pulled her arm back as far as she could and then brought it forward quickly, smacking John square in the middle of the back with the leather straps and the metal beads that were attached to her whip.

"Aaaaaaggggghhhh! Shit! Yesss!" John yelled and Alexis smirked with pleasure. She pulled her arms back once more and brought it forward again, with great precision, and smacked John once again on the back. Her blow was a little higher this time and some of the beads smashed into the base of John's neck.

"Aaaaaaaagh! Oh my God!" Alexis' smile grew wider as she saw the redness blot up on John's body. She was having the time of her life.

Months ago, she was pregnant from a man that had raped her. Not just any man, but her best friend from college. He was one of the few men on Earth that she felt like she could trust and be herself with, but she found out that he was not at all what she thought. It took her a minute to get herself together. Took a while for her to work through all of the pain and the guilt that she felt, not to mention the constant "dirty" feeling. She felt like her skin oozed the scent of semen, sex, and hopelessness.

Once she was able to work through her issues, she knew that her next stop was to the clinic. Although her friends had told her that it was a possibility that the baby belonged to her husband, Marc. She knew that whole line of thinking was bullshit. She had been married to Marc for five years and used no protection. Not once did she get pregnant. As far as she was concerned, he'd had a gun full of blanks that he'd been shooting in her for five whole years. There was no way he could have been the father.

Alexis' sister, Vanessa had been the one to take her to the clinic. Although Alexis was sure that Vanessa and Marc had been sleeping together when she had finally returned home from being raped, Vanessa had denied that to the end. She stated that she had been about to have sex with Marc, but he resisted. Alexis still couldn't understand why Vanessa would even try to sleep with her own sister's husband, but she did attempt at some half-ass excuse.

"I'm so so sorry for what happened with Marc, Lex. The love that he has for you. It reminded me of someone that I...someone who loved me very much. Someone that I lost. I'm sorry, Alexis.

Alexis pulled back her arm and slammed the whip back down onto John's chest. He yelped loudly and then she threw down her whip. She placed her foot into his back and dug her heel down hard.

"You like that?" She yelled through clenched teeth. Her nipples were getting hard as she watched him squirm from underneath her. The feel of being the dominant one excited her.

"Uuuughhh! Yes! I love it." John yelled out. He was enjoying it so much that he was slobbering and there was a damp spot growing out from under his face on the bed sheets.

"Get the fuck up and lick my stilettos." Alexis said pulling back for John to fumble his way off the bed. He scurried up from the bed so fast that he almost tripped over his own feet.

After Vanessa had apologized, Alexis was too emotionally drained to continue to worry about it. She had other issues and she felt the important thing to note was that you can't trust a hoe around your man. Shortly after, Vanessa spoke to her about the baby. Vanessa advised her that if she didn't want it, she only had a limited amount of time to get rid of it. Alexis knew that Vanessa the process. Alexis had to accompany Vanessa to the clinic to get an abortion when she was sixteen years old. Vanessa never told her who the father was, but it was a very emotional experience for her. Alexis was positive that it wouldn't be the same for her, though. A quick drive to the clinic and Alexis had gotten rid of her problem and she didn't even feel bad. In fact, she felt nothing. Nothing except anger.

Alexis had anger that she didn't have an outlet for. Her life had been so full of faking perfection and being the trophy wife to a man who had no clue that she didn't even know how to deal with this new part of her personality. It wasn't until she was going for a check-up following the abortion that she met Sharonda.

Sharonda was a woman who appeared younger than Alexis, but something about her vibe let you know that she was mentally much older than she looked. Alexis was at her check-up appointment alone and she was seething. Everyone she came into contact with was getting the Queen Bitch attitude that she had been handing out since the abortion. She had nothing to do to get rid of all the fury that she had in her so she directed it at any and everyone.

Alexis had been sitting with her legs crossed, tapping her nails against the armrest of her chair waiting for her name to be called to see the doctor. She was annoyed and it was not a secret. Her appointment was for 1:45 and it was damn near 2:20 and her name had not been called. Sharonda walked in and sat right next to Alexis. Not two chairs down. Not in front of her. *Right next to her*, although the entire room was empty. That pissed Alexis off.

Alexis turned to sneer at Sharonda and instead of the girl's response being one of fear or attitude; Sharonda gave her a knowing look as if she understood. It threw Alexis off a little, but she continued to glare at her.

"What are you looking at, bitch?" Alexis growled under her breath. Sharonda didn't look surprised or offended. Instead she smirked back at her.

"So, what happened? Boyfriend fuck you and leave? You found out he had a wife? Ohh....you got pregnant from some nigga who gave you a STD?" Her response alarmed Alexis and she immediately grew embarrassed. She ducked her head in shame. That was when Sharonda knew. "Rape...?" She whispered. Alexis wasn't sure what it was about the girl that made her want to confess, but she did. She sat there in the waiting area of the clinic and shared a secret with a complete stranger. A secret that she hadn't even told her best friends or her husband. The rest that followed was nearly a blur. Sharonda had introduced her to a woman who she said could assist her with her anger: Ms. Juice.

Ms. Juice ran a business of a particular nature, but it was a thriving business. It was a place where whether you were male or female, you could get your fantasies carried out. So many men and women frequented the large business that it was a wonder that she hadn't been caught by the Feds yet. Actually...it wasn't that much of a wonder since some of her top clients were apart of the FBI.

When Alexis first met Ms. Juice, she thought that Sharonda was crazy for bringing her. She didn't understand how sex with anyone could make her feel better, especially when sex had been the basis of her problem to begin with. However, Ms. Juice showed her that the same thing that had been used to try to destroy her could be used to create her power. And that's what she did.

"Get up!" Alexis yelled. She lifted her foot and nudged John backwards across the room by his forehead. She didn't know what his name really was and she didn't really care. In her mind, they were all Johns. She watched as John rolled over to his side and struggled to his feet. She twisted up her face in disgust. He was so weak. So stupid and so worthless. He probably had a wife and children at home waiting on him, but instead he enjoyed coming over and getting his ass beat. Alexis closed her eyes and let out a deep, throaty laugh. When she opened her eyes again, she noticed John was looking at her with a confused look on his face.

"What are you still doing here? Get up and get out. Leave my tip on the counter. And it better be more than that lil shit you left me last time." Alexis said as she walked over to the door that led to her private room. It was late; her day of work was done. It was time to take a shower, go home and be a wife.

"WHAT'S FOR DINNER?" MARC ASKED AS HE LOOKING INTO THE bedroom. Alexis was lying in the bed reading. She looked like the definition of comfortable. She had her head propped up on pillows and one leg was resting atop the knee of the other. She had one hand holding a book and the other arm was behind her, providing support to her head. She was at ease. Which is the exact reason why she didn't understand why Marc's mouth was moving and interrupting her present state of calm.

"I don't know. What did you cook?" Alexis asked placing her book down on the side of the bed.

"Uh....nothing. What do you mean?" Marc looked genuinely confused. Alexis just stared at him, without saying a word. He had been home all day and she had been away.

Nigga, why didn't you cook? She thought. She rolled her eyes; picked her book back up and started back reading. Marc waited for a little while and then walked away from the door. She was just about to get back to the good part when her phone rang. She picked up her cell and looked at the name on the caller id. It was Kaylen.

"Hello?" Alexis said as she put the bookmark into her book. It was apparent that it was not meant for her to finish that chapter at the moment.

"Hey, girl...what's been happening? It's been a few days since I heard from you. Shit, a few weeks since I've seen you. What have you been up to?" Alexis smiled before she responded. She had missed her friends, but it was hard to keep up with them since she had been spending most of her time at Ms. Juice's spot. Kaylen and Jazmyn did not know about her involvement with Ms. Juice and she wanted to keep it that way, so it had been a while since they'd caught up with each other.

"Hey...yeah, it has been a while. I haven't been doing too much, honestly. Just a little resting and taking it easy. What about you and Caleb?"

"Oh, it's all fine with him. I've been going over the wedding details. No date yet though." Kaylen said slowly. Her voice was light and airy, just like it normally was when she was lying. Alexis rolled her eyes upward while she held the phone.

"Why are you marrying that clown again?" Alexis sighed heavily.

"Alexis!" Kaylen yelled into the phone.

"Look, I'm sorry, Kay. But he is not exactly marriage material." Alexis paused and thought about what she said.

I guess I'm not marriage material anymore either.

"Caleb is different now. You will see." Alexis almost snorted with laughter. The way that Kaylen said it was so unbelievable. There was no way that she even believed the words that came out of her own mouth. She didn't even *sound* sincere. Alexis was about to point that out when she stopped herself. There was no need to tell Kaylen anything more about it. Caleb was sure to show his true self sometime soon.

She will find out sooner than later, Alexis thought to herself.

"Well, Kay, I don't mean to cut the conversation short, but I really need to go now," Alexis lied. The only thing she had to get back to was her book, but Kaylen's men problems were very far from what she wanted to hear at the moment. If she couldn't tell that Caleb was a joke, then Alexis didn't know who could.

"Ok, Lexi. I will call you again soon." With that, Alexis hung up the phone without saying 'bye' and picked up her book again.

KAYLEN

$\mathcal{K}$aylen hung up the phone and tried to get rid of the concern that she'd felt for her friend. Alexis had experienced something that no woman should have ever had to go through and although she didn't seem to be in as bad of a state as she was initially, she was definitely changed. What made Kaylen feel worse is that, she'd felt that she was partially responsible for what had happened to her. The night of Zo's party, Kaylen had a feeling that she should have intervened when she saw Alexis and Dexter kissing and touching on each other, but then she became so wrapped up in her own drama with Salem that she'd forgotten all about Alexis.

Salem. The thought of him still sent chills down Kaylen's spine. She had always thought that Post-Traumatic Stress Disorder was a joke, but she knew now that it wasn't the case. Kaylen was still terrified of being in a completely dark room and any room that was totally enclosed. It reminded her of the days and nights that she spent alone in the basement either cooking meth or waiting for Salem to return with more ingredients.

Kaylen flicked the switch in her car to turn on her blinker towards home. Actually Caleb's home. He wanted her to move in with him, but she had too much going on to be able to do that at the moment. After she was arrested for Salem's murder, the next call that Caleb had made was to Jazmyn. He knew her and he was certain that she was the best one to get Kaylen out of jail. Sure enough, within 24 hours, Kaylen was released from jail on bond. About two months later, they stated that they were dropping the case against her altogether. Kaylen wasn't sure why, and she didn't care. The only important thing to her was that she was no longer in fear of losing her freedom for a murder she had not committed.

As she pulled up to the yard, she hit the switch to make the garage door open. She pulled her car up next to Caleb's and killed the engine. Caleb had taken her lack of response to his proposal as an automatic "yes" and Kaylen failed to tell him otherwise even after she'd been released from jail. Everything had been happening too quickly and she hadn't really had any time to respond. Now here it was about five months after the proposal and, even though she hadn't moved into the house with him, she was wearing the ring.

It's what's best for now. Kaylen had been telling herself that for a while now. Moving out of her townhome may have been a good idea. All she could think about for the first few weeks after she'd returned home was the last night she had spent there before Salem kidnapped her and what had occurred with Zo. Every time she thought of him, she felt a sharp pang in her chest. She hadn't seen or spoke to him since the night that he'd shot Salem.

When she was released from jail, she thought she saw him in the parking lot, but she wasn't sure if she had or if her mind was playing horrible tricks on her. Caleb pulled up to her and she jumped in his car, but the hairs on the back of her neck had stood on end, making her feel as if she was being watched. One day she found the nerve to call him but she had been sent directly to voicemail after one ring. She took that as a hint that Zo didn't want to have anything else to do with her. Kaylen couldn't blame him. Messing with her had ruined their friendship and eventually

Kaylen collected her things and got out of her car. She pulled out her key to unlock the door, but before she could, the door swung open.

"Hey, sweetie. How was class?" Caleb said, pulling her into a hug. Kaylen wrapped her arms around Caleb and returned the embrace. She kissed him gently on the cheek before releasing him.

"It was fine. The material is a little challenging, but I'm making it through." Kaylen walked to the pantry and pulled out a bag of chips. She opened the bag and popped one into her mouth.

"Well, we need to talk, but that can wait for later. You look really sexy for someone just trying to get to class." Caleb said coming up behind her and wrapping his arms around her front. Kaylen squirmed slightly as she felt Caleb reached under her short skirt and slip her panties to the side. His sexual desire was insatiable, but it made sense. Caleb was used to have multiple women at one time so he was also used to constant pleasure.

While Kaylen wasn't used to multiple lovers, she was used to good sex so she opened up her legs a little to allow for Caleb to get full access. He dipped his middle finger into her warmth and then curved it and began a flicking motion inside of her while he used his forefinger to stroke her clit. Then sensation made Kaylen's knees go weak and she allowed Caleb's body to support her from behind. He pulled his other arm underneath her and then scooped her up in his arms making sure to keep his middle fingers snuggled deep within her. Kaylen relaxed and let her legs fall open as he started to carry her to their bedroom.

Kaylen moaned as Caleb started kissing her on her neck while he held her. He inserted two more fingers into her and she felt her body shuddering.

"No." Caleb said as he flipped her and placed her down at the base of the stairs. He pulled his fingers out and pushed her legs apart.

"What are you doing?" Kaylen asked him breathlessly.

"I can't wait." Caleb said as he pulled at the buttons on her shirt. She relaxed back on the stairs and allowed him to free her breast. She quietly thanked God that she wore a bra that opened from the front. Caleb dropped his pants and pushed her legs open with his body as he rubbed his throbbing manhood against her. He dipped his head low and licked around the outside of one of her nipples. Kaylen moaned as the heat from his mouth mixed with the cool of the air and teased her skin.

Caleb pushed harder against her as he sucked in her entire nipple and began to suck gently.

"Oh, shiiii...." Kaylen breathed out slowly as she felt her other nipple tightening up. Caleb reached over and grabbed it tightly between his two fingers and squeezed. It made Kaylen's clit harden and she gasped out of pleasure and twitched against his hard dick. She felt the moisture from her pussy soak up the material on Caleb's boxers as he pushed closer into her. He continued pinching her nipple tightly as he raised his head and started sucking on her neck. Kaylen let her head drop to the side in absolute ecstasy as she tried her best to endure the intensity of pleasure she was feeling.

"You're ready?" He asked her softly against her neck.

"No. Sit your ass down on the stairs." She said gently and she moved over to the side, making Caleb's fingers slide out of her. Her panties fell back in place and she soaked them up immediately. She stood up partially as she allowed Caleb to kick off his pants, which were draped around his ankles, and lay back on the stairs. Kaylen crossed over and turned so that she hovered on top of him. Then she released his hardness from the slit in the front of his boxers. The warmth from his pulsating dick excited her and she felt her panties clutching to the inside of her pussy lips from the moisture she released.

"Hmmmm....." Caleb moaned as Kaylen blew cold air onto the head of his dick. This was the part of their intimacy that she enjoyed the most. She enjoyed sucking on Caleb because she knew it pleased him and he always wanted more. She loved his reaction to her gentle sucks and kisses on the tip of his dick. Kaylen lifted it up and slid her tongue up and down the underside of the shaft like a pro. Her tongue and twisted around it like an acrobat twirling in the air. She looked up and saw Caleb hang his head back and squeeze his eyes shut. He got harder than she imagined he could and she was able to see the pre-cum rise up out of his dick. She felt his whole body tense up as every muscle reacted to the extreme pleasure that his main member was receiving.

"Damn, baby...oh, shit!" Caleb said as Kaylen placed her mouth gently on the head and created a vacuum with her lips. She sucked gently at first just on the tip and then took the fullness of him in her mouth. She heard Caleb's breathing quicken as she went up and down on him. She filled her mouth up with saliva and let it drip all over him.

"Damn...Kay, you better stop that shit." Caleb said quietly. Kaylen pulled her head up and blew once again onto his dick. She sat up before pulling her panties to the side and the next sensation that he felt was her warm pussy folding around him. Kaylen wiggled a little in order to take in all of him before she began rotating her hips on him in slow motion. She then started moving up and down, making sure to go up from the base to the tip. Caleb grabbed her ass and tried to control the motion, but Kaylen wasn't having that. She started bouncing faster and he squeezed hard on her ass as if he was trying to make it burst.

Caleb's mouth fell open in ecstasy and his body relaxed and went limp as he let Kaylen enjoy herself. But then, all of a sudden, she felt him arch forward suddenly and push deeper into her. Kaylen gasped as she felt him go in deeper than she had ever felt before.

"Uh, huh...thought you was about to run this dick, huh?" Caleb smiled, showing his pearly white teeth that set nicely against his dark brown skin. With one quick motion, he flipped Kaylen over on her back and held her up from behind with one hand so that her back wasn't lying totally on the stairs. He steadied himself using the banister and thrust forward into her hard.

"Oh, yessss....." Kaylen moaned. Caleb bent down towards her and started biting gently on her nipple while he thrust again and again into her soaking wet pussy. Kaylen's mouth opened and she wrapped her legs around Caleb's waist tightly, pulling him in closer.

"Caleb, come with me...please." She gasped as she felt the orgasm rising up from the tips of her toes. It was erupting through her in waves and she knew the biggest ripple was on its way. She braced herself against him as she tried to control the tide. She wanted to wait for Caleb to come with her.

"No..." was Caleb's simple response. He continued pumping and Kaylen dug her nails into her back as she felt the pleasure intensifying.

"I can't hold it, baby. Pleeeeeaaasssse..."

"Do it, Kay!" Caleb urged. Kaylen wasted no time complying with his request. She couldn't hold it any longer. Her orgasm washed over her and she shuddered at the feeling.

"Ugggggghhhh, Shiiiiitttttttt!" She dug her nails deeper into him and pressed closer into him.

"Daamn, Kay. Mmmhmmmm...."" Caleb said up against the base of her neck. She felt Caleb's dick contracting in her and she knew that he had reached his pleasure peak as well. Thank God for birth control because the warm liquid that Caleb pumped into her seemed to have no ending. Kaylen held tightly onto him and enjoyed the feel of him breathing against her neck.

Suddenly, Caleb shifted and began to stand up. He cradled her gently and pulled her up with him. Kaylen nestled her head up against him as she allowed him to walk her up the stairs. She felt remnants of his love dripping from her and she clenched her lady lips together while she gripped him around the neck. Once in their master bedroom, Caleb dropped her gently onto the bed. He pulled the covers up around her and kissed her gently on the cheek.

"Take your ass to sleep, Kay." He said patting her softly.

"Mmmmhhmmmm. You know me so well, baby." Kaylen said yawning as she closed her eyes and let exhaustion takeover.

A FEW HOURS LATER, KAYLEN OPENED HER EYES AND SQUINTED AT THE sunlight. She looked over at the clock on her nightstand. It was 3:00 o'clock in the afternoon. Her stomach growled and her mouth felt dry as if were made of sandpaper. She rolled over, half-expecting Caleb to be in the bed in her, but all she was greeted with was a vacant spot. She pulled the covers off and walked over to the walk-in closet to grab her robe. She walked slowly down the stairs and sped up her pace once she heard Caleb in the living room. She walked pass him and to the pantry to look for something to snack on.

"Hungry?"

"Yeah, but there is nothing to...." Kaylen was about to turn to face Caleb when she noticed luggage stacked next to the door leading to the garage.

"Going somewhere?" Kaylen asked, raising her eyebrows at Caleb. He hadn't mentioned anything before she left the house that morning or throughout the day.

"Uh...yes, actually, that's what I said I needed to speak to you about earlier. I have to go out to LA. I need to leave tonight." Caleb said nonchalantly. Kaylen knew that as a medical professor that Caleb often had to travel for seminars and to teach first year medical students or speak at events, but he had not done any of this since he had asked her to marry him.

Although Kaylen had not officially accepted his proposal, she'd gone along with it as well as the relationship. She had wanted for so long to be Caleb's official girlfriend that once she was given the opportunity, though at the worst of times, she readily accepted the role. Caleb had been so attentive to her that she felt that he had changed his philandering ways. There were no late night phone calls from other women, no women had showed up at the front door when she was over there, and Caleb had not been suspiciously texting at all hours of the night, so Kaylen figured he really was serious about her this time. This trip out of town was very unexpected and Kaylen was a little apprehensive. She had wondered how long it would take for Caleb to drop back into the lifestyle he was accustomed to.

"Why are you just now telling me?" Kaylen asked as she walked to the refrigerator to grab a bottle of water. Caleb sat down at the bar and watched her.

"I just found out. You remember me telling you about Nikki, right? She had another ticket to this conference that I have wanted to go to. Apparently, one of her friends was going to go with her, but she got sick at the last minute. She called me and told me that I could have the extra ticket." Kaylen rolled her eyes. Nikki had been trying to get with Caleb for the longest and he would have to be the absolute dumbest man on Earth if he had no idea.

"Really?" Kaylen asked sarcastically. "Her friend just happened to get sick, huh?"

"Kay, it's not even like that. You have nothing to worry about." Kaylen looked at Caleb in his eyes and she struggled to believe him. In the past, Caleb had never lied about his shit. In the days when he did not want to commit, he did not hide that fact. Although he was always a gentleman with how he treated her, he'd never lied and told her that she was the only one or that he wanted to be exclusive. Kaylen wanted to believe that Caleb had turned over a new leaf and that he was a new person like he said he was. He said that he was into her and wanted only her and she wanted to believe that. But something about him wanting to hang out with "big booty Nikki" didn't sit right with her at all.

"Well, when will you be back?" Kaylen asked as she untwisted the cap to the water. She kept her eyes focused on Caleb as she took a long gulp of the icy liquid.

"It's a four day conference, so I will be back by Saturday at the latest." Kaylen almost choked on her water.

It's a four day conference, but you won't be back until Saturday. Does this nigga think I can't count? Today is Sunday!

"If you are leaving today, shouldn't you be back by Thursday if it's a four day conference?" Kaylen eyed Caleb suspiciously.

"Well...yes. But it doesn't officially start until Tuesday; tomorrow we have some meet and greet sessions. Also, I have some other things that I need to take care of before I get back here." Caleb said before jumping up from the barstool to give her a kiss on the cheek. "Look, baby, I have to head over to the airport before I miss my flight. I will give you a call when I get in. Love you, Kay."

"Love you, too, Caleb." Kaylen mumbled as she watched Caleb drag his luggage out of the door.

Kaylen picked up her cellphone and dialed Jazmyn's number. She knew that Alexis was not in a position to hear about any of her issues, so she hoped that Jazmyn was free to listen to hers. Unfortunately, it didn't seem as if that was the case because after a few rings, she heard the voicemail pick up.

"Damn it!" Kaylen yelled slamming the cellphone on the counter. Jazmyn had been a hard person to reach for the past few months, but Kaylen was hoping that she would have been able to speak to her. If anyone could tell if someone was cheating, it was Jaz. She had been involved in so many cheating scandals in her lifetime, that she had a cheater radar on her and she could sniff another cheater out a mile away.

Kaylen sat down in her favorite leather recliner in the sitting room. She closed her eyes and tried to erase the doubts she had concerning Caleb out of her mind.

I can't deal with any more of these damn secrets! I've had enough of this shit, Kaylen thought. After putting up with Salem's sneaking around to get high and then finding out that he was a full blown addict, Kaylen wasn't sure that her mind could deal with another man with secrets. She needed her life to be as drama free as possible.

JAZMYN

I killed your mama, little girl. I killed your mama. Jazmyn cradled LaShea as she rocked her gently to sleep. The little girl was resisting as much as she could, but Jazmyn was determined to get the baby to sleep. As she grew impatient, her rocking became a little faster. La'Shea gave her a look as if to ask "you crazy?" and Jazmyn slowed down a little.

"Is she asleep yet?" Kingston whispered through the bedroom door.

"Almost." Jazmyn mouthed back. She turned her attention back to the baby and continued to rock her as she saw her eyelids flicker closed.

Five months ago, Jazmyn had seen this room for the first time. Although Jazmyn felt the need to change the décor of the room once she moved in, it still reminded her of the day that she first stepped in it when she was on her way to give Shanice what was due to her. Jazmyn felt a smile creeping up at the edges of her mouth as she thought back to that day. Once Shanice was gone, she was able to get everything she wanted. Shanice was gone and her and Kingston were together. No one knew who LaShea's father was, so she was able to stay with Kingston and Jazmyn took care of her as her own.

"Everyone got a better life as soon as that bitch was gone." Jazmyn whispered to herself. She took one last look at LaShea before placing her gently into her crib. Jazmyn backed slowly out of the room and closed the door behind her. She walked over to the bedroom next door where Kingston was lying down.

"Join me?" Kingston asked, patting the side of the bed.

"Actually, I can't. I have to head out. I have some work to do." Jazmyn said as she pulled off her black sweatpants and sweatshirt. She grabbed a nice pantsuit from the closet and pulled the pants over her slim hips.

"Again? When am I going to see the new office?" Kingston asked sitting up on the bed. He dipped his head to the side and Jazmyn couldn't help feeling a little aroused by his stare.

"Soon." Jazmyn lied. Kingston would never be able to see where she worked.

Better not to have him ask too many questions.

"Well, baby, I was kinda hoping we could get into something while the baby is sleeping." Kingston said patting his crotch. He had a sexy grin on his face and it made Jazmyn get moist immediately. She eyed the bulge in his pants and sighed.

"When I get back, baby. I promise." Jazmyn leaned over to give Kingston a light kiss on the lips before grabbing her briefcase and running out of the room.

"But Jaz…"

"Kingston, I promise!" Jazmyn yelled back before closing the door behind her.

"AAAAARRRRRGGGGHHHHH!!" Jazmyn bashed the backside of her 9mm into Isaac's head one more time and watched as the blood trickled slowly down the back of his neck like hot wax on a burning candle. Dom snickered in the background as he watched. He loved to see Jazmyn in action. When him and Crimson had asked her to return to the business, they thought it would take some time for her to become the killer they had trained her to be, but they were wrong. Jazmyn came back with a vengeance and it took no time at all for her to go back to being the cold blooded animal that they had bred for situations such as these. The truth was that Jazmyn had so much pent up anger and frustration that it was easy for her to fall back in place. Dealing with Kingston had put her in a place where she was poised and ready to slice any nigga up that fell out of line. No questions asked.

"I didn't do nothing, I swear. It wasn't me. I wouldn't ever mess with the clique like that!" The man blubbered at her feet. He was breathing on borrowed time and Jazmyn was ready to rectify the situation.

The pile of pussy at her feet was someone by the name of Isaac. Dom had called her earlier that day and told her that he had suspected that Isaac had been stealing from one of the stash houses, but with the installation of some new security cameras, it had been confirmed about an hour ago. Once Jazmyn got the text that death was pending for this fool, she was only too happy to be of assistance. Loyalty was everything and one less disloyal motherfucker walking the Earth would make it a better place.

"You wanna live, motherfucker?" Jazmyn hissed kicking Isaac in the stomach. Isaac nodded his head wildly as he coughed and spewed up blood all over the floor in front of him. The scene in front of them made Dom double over in laughter. "I don't think you do. Show me how much you wanna live." Isaac looked up at Jazmyn with a confused expression. She turned and looked at Dom. "Dom, take that dick out. If you really wanna live, pussy nigga, go suck his dick."

Jazmyn stepped back and watched as Isaac tried his best to scoot over to where Dom stood. As he slid along the floor, he left a trail of blood behind him. With much struggle, he was finally able to reach Dom's feet. He stopped to lift his head and was immediately met with size 13 shoes to the skull as Dom kicked the shit out of him. Jazmyn bent over with laughter as she watched.

"Faggot ass nigga! Get the fuck away from me!" Isaac winced as he tried to back away from Dom when he raised his foot again. Jazmyn doubled over with laughter, she could barely compose herself.

"Jaz, slice this nigga up right now! You a *nasty* ass motherfucker. My niggas are expected to go out like a G to the end and you ready to suck a dick to save your shitty ass life. Finish him up, and make that shit slow." Dom twisted up his face in disgust before walking out of the warehouse. Jazmyn smiled and pulled out her smallest blade as she watched Isaac shivering on the floor from fear.

"So I heard you got sticky fingers. You like to take stuff that ain't yours, huh? What you think I should do about that?"

"No, man....I told you I ain't do shit!" Isaac blubbered as he tried to move away from her glare. It only made Jazmyn hate him even more. She didn't understand how these niggas could be vetted into the crew as certified killers and then become pussies as soon as shit hit the fan. Annoyed, Jazmyn pulled back out her gun, reached back behind her head and then swung forward as fast as she could, slamming the butt of her 9mm down onto Isaac's right eye.

"AAAAARRRRRGGGHHH!!!!" Isaac yelled right before he started writhing on the floor as if he were having a seizure.

"I told your ass before that I ain't no motherfucking man!" Jazmyn yelled before bringing her hand down again and knocking him in the other eye. Isaac stopped moving, but he was still breathing loudly. It seemed almost as if he was paralyzed with fear.

After pulling on her gloves, Jazmyn grabbed her blade, squatted down and grabbed one of Isaac's fingers that were now turning gray at the tips. One quick motion and she cut off the top section of his finger, splitting his fingernail and most of the flesh underneath from the base of his finger. Isaac began convulsing and a blood and saliva mix started spewing from his mouth. A strong, repulsing smell hit Jazmyn's nose and it made her back up. She covered her nose and mouth with her sleeve.

"Damn! Did this nigga....ahhh, hell! This nigga done shitted himself!" Jazmyn grabbed her gun out of the holster on her back and aimed it at his skull. One to the head, two to the chest and she was done. She turned around and made her way quickly out of the warehouse.

"Thought I told you to make that shit slow, Jay." Dom said, leaning on the front of his all black Hummer truck. The rims shined like diamonds in the sunlight along with all the platinum chains that he was determined to wear. There was no mistaking that Dom was the boss of something big. Few people knew just how big. Dom was mixed up in things that black folks usually didn't even bother to deal with. But in his mind, everyone had an addiction and, whatever it was; he was willing to supply it.

"That nigga shitted himself. You know I don't deal with that." Jazmyn said walking around Dom to jump in the passenger seat. "I'm about to call the clean-up crew to take care of the rest of that." Dom jumped in the driver's side and started the car.

"How you handled that nigga in there made my dick hard." Dom grinned over at Jazmyn and winked. She rolled her eyes at him before erupting in laughter.

"Don't even start with me, Dom. You know this ain't what you want." Jazmyn looked at him while licking her lips sexily. Now it was Dom's turn to laugh.

"You still messing around with that lawyer?" Just that quickly the conversation got serious. Jazmyn hated how Dom could go from shits and giggles to serious business in less than two seconds. She had been trying to keep her personal relationship with Kingston under wraps because she knew that Crimson and Dom wouldn't approve. She knew they would think that her relationship with Kingston was too risky, given the fact that she had murdered his wife. Not to mention the fact that she was now playing mommy to Shanice's daughter.

"I'm still seeing him, yes. But you know I'm careful..." Jazmyn started.

"Fuck that, Jay. You should know by now that you can never be careful enough. You better watch your back because you know what you will have to do if this shit goes sour." Dom was facing forward, but Jazmyn saw him glance at her out of the side of his eyes.

He wouldn't ask me to kill Kingston, would he? Jazmyn thought, but she already knew the answer. Dom didn't hesitate to off anyone that became a threat. And even if there was divine intervention and Dom wanted to spare someone, Crimson was always there to veto the decision. There was never divine intervention when it concerned Crimson, because she had no soul.

"I'm not trying to tell you what to do with your personal shit because that ain't my style. But if it starts becoming my business....you know the deal." Dom said as he rounded the corner to where she had left her car. He stopped right behind her all-black Mercedes Benz and pressed the button to unlock the door. Jazmyn jumped out without saying a word and Dom didn't even turn to look at her. He was pissed and she knew it, but he also respected her and that was the only reason that he hadn't already had someone get rid of her. Before she could even walk over to her car, Dom sped off down the road.

Jazmyn let out a heavy sigh and pressed the button to unlock her door. She sat down in the seat and pulled out her cellphone to call Kingston. It wasn't until she started the car that she heard the beeping.

"What the fuck?" Jazmyn said before snatching off her seatbelt and jumping out of the car. She had barely been able to run down to the next intersection before she heard the explosion. She turned around and saw her car go up in flames. The noise of the blast seemed to be enough to wake the whole city. The sound echoed loudly in her ears even a few seconds after the initial blast.

Jazmyn grabbed at the sides of her face in distress as she gawked at what was left of her vehicle. People in the neighborhood began to look out of their windows and some even walked out of their front doors to see what was going on. Jazmyn could see that some people were even on their cellphones...most likely making calls to the police. It was at that moment that she decided it was time to get lost. She already knew that if Crimson and Dom were behind this, they had already gotten rid of all identifying information from her vehicle before they put the bomb in it, so there was no way the police would be able to trace it. Jazmyn pulled out her cellphone and dialed the number of a car service that she used in her previous life to pick up her clients.

How the hell am I going to explain this to Kingston? Jazmyn had so many thoughts swirling around in her head, but none of them concerned any level of surprise at what had just occurred. Dom wanted her to know that he meant what he said and although she'd understood his message clear enough the first time, it was crystal clear now. She just had to figure out how she was going to protect Kingston through all of this.

"Where am I taking you?" the driver said to Jazmyn once he had arrived. He was an older man with dark brown skin. His hair was brown with flecks of gray in it and his teeth were pure white. He had a large smile on his face and Jazmyn watched him as he looked her up and down quickly. She sucked her teeth when he let his eyes linger around her breasts.

"Just keep heading straight down this road. I will let you know when to stop." Jazmyn said staring at the man through his rearview mirror. He seemed to not be aware of the fact that she was looking at him because he continued to let his eyes fall onto her chest area.

"You wanna lose those eyes?" Jazmyn sneered at the man. His eyes shot up and he met her glare. One look let him know that she meant business. Jazmyn let him drive on for about ten minutes before she told him tapped on the window.

"Stop here." The driver stopped and Jazmyn threw him a $20 bill. She usually gave a bigger tip to drivers but she didn't think this man deserved it. Jazmyn got out of the car and made sure to slam the door extra hard before walking the rest of the way to Kingston's house. Although she still kept her townhouse, she spent the majority of her time with Kingston. He had asked her plenty of times to move in, but she had a hard time making the decision to move in with him when she had so many secrets that she needed to keep him from finding out about. She also wanted to protect him as much as she could from getting caught on Dom and Crimson's radar. When Jazmyn turned the corner and Kingston's home came into view, what she saw chilled her to the bone.

There sitting in the driveway as if it had never left, was her car. Jazmyn squinted as she tried to get a better look. She thought that maybe her eyes had been playing tricks on her. She jogged the rest of the way to the house and stopped once she reached the all black Mercedes S-class sedan. It *looked* like hers, but once Jazmyn was close to it, she could tell it wasn't. This car was much, much better. Jazmyn tried the door and noticed that it was unlocked. She sat down in the driver's side and admired the smooth, cool, black leather seats and the wood grain interior. Her car had been nice and had all the upgrades, but this one was definitely top of the line.

Jazmyn was about to get out of the car and walk into the house when she felt a vibration from below her. She reached back and grabbed her cellphone from out of her back pocket.

You like? As Jazmyn read the message, she felt the anxiety rise up starting from the back of her neck and extending, like fingers, out through the rest of her body.

Crimson.

ALEXIS

"Alexis, how are you doing today?" Ms. Juice was sitting at her humongous cherry wood desk with her elbows resting on the top and her hands clasped together. Alexis eyed her curiously and sat down in the chair in front of the desk. Ms. Juice had asked her to come in and meet with her and Alexis had no idea why. She hadn't had a private conversation with Ms. Juice since the time that she first came in and discussed what had happened to her. Since then, she had left Alexis to do whatever she needed to do. There hadn't been any complaints from any Johns so Alexis didn't understand what the issue was.

"What do we need to speak about?" Alexis said tossing her hair over her shoulder. She had dyed her auburn hair and made it bleach blond. It was a huge change and Marc had looked at her with a blank and confused stare for days, but it fit her. Once she began wearing the dark eyeliner to go along with it, Marc walked around with a constant erection, but for some reason, he hadn't even tried to touch her once in the months that passed since the incident.

"I wanted to speak to you about your work here." Ms. Juice sat back in her seat, but her hands remained clasped together as she rested her elbows on the armrests of her chair. The older woman had hair that looked as if she had tried to dye it black to cover her gray, but she'd only succeeded in making her gray's turn a dark blue-ish color. She still managed to make her look appear classy by having her hair pulled back tightly into a neat bun. Her make-up was excellent and Alexis admired her ability to make herself seem perfectly put together everyday regardless of the hour. The house was open 24 hours and Ms. Juice managed to always be around and still look as if she had been able to have a full day's rest before arriving to work for the day.

"You have been able to let off steam by performing your preferred acts of torture with a select few of our clients. However, we have other clients, high paying clients, who have expressed interest in you. I expect everyone here to be versatile and pull their weight. I under-stand that you aren't doing this for money...that you need to let off steam, but you are still taking up a room in this house to explore your fetishes and I need you to bring in enough money to cover the room that you are occupying. I could easily throw someone in there who is willing to go the whole way and bring in double what you bring in. So if you intend on staying, you need to be a little more.....flexible."

Ms. Juice pursed her lips together as she looked back at Alexis. Her lips were pushed together so tightly that Alexis could see the cracks in her dark red lipstick. Alexis did not flinch, did not move and did not change at all, other than to narrow her eyes in on Ms. Juice's smug expression. She seemed to take pleasure in the fact that she had the authority to demand someone to give over their body to another person so that she could profit. Her dark skin appeared to lighten with pleasure and her high cheeks bones rose even higher as she delighted in her ridiculous request.

Nothing makes this bitch smile wider than the thought of money.

"I will *not* allow anyone to touch me like that," Alexis said through her teeth. She watched as Ms. Juice's face changed and she revealed her signature "I run shit so comply or get out" smirk. It made Alexis' blood begin to boil. She didn't work for Ms. Juice for the money, but she did have a reason that she worked at the house and she wanted to be able to continue.

"Listen, Alexis. You don't really have a choice. I know you find what you do to men here to be therapeutic, but I'm not running a rehabilitation center or a psychiatric ward. I have some top clients who are willing to pay me for time with you, so you can either agree to do what I need for you to do or you can get the fuck out and settle your post-rape issues elsewhere." Alexis flinched at Ms. Juice words. She wasn't sure how to react or what to say. What she did know was that she needed to continue what she had started here.

"You want me to start having sex with them...now?" Alexis asked slowly.

"No, not now. The man that asked about you is out of town for now. When he returns, you better be ready. He is a top payer and I won't have you fucking shit up for me." With that, Alexis got up and started to walk to the door.

"Where are you going? I didn't tell you to move!" Ms. Juice hissed as she rose from her seat.

"To my room. I have clients." Alexis sneered back at the woman. She was trying to control her anger. At the moment she just really wanted to smack the shit out of her, but she figured she would reserve that for John.

"Think long and hard about what I said, Alexis." Ms. Juice said just as Alexis walked out and slammed the door behind her. She resisted the urge to tell Ms. Juice to stick something "long and hard" straight up her ass.

Not trying to hear that bullshit.

Alexis walked into her room and went back in towards her dressing room. She pulled off the dress that she had been wearing. She threw it on a chair and went over the closet to pull out something to wear that was better suited for what she was getting ready to do. She had a lot of steam to blow off this time and she needed something that would assist by making her feel powerful. She finally settled on a pair of short black leather shorts and a red leather bra.

Alexis was just about to pull the shorts up around her hips when she heard her cellphone chime.

"Probably Marc." She groaned to herself. It was beginning to be harder and harder to avoid him. He was growing suspicious by her need to leave the house everyday for hours at a time. Alexis didn't care enough about his concerns or questions to even provide an explanation. Her phone chirped again and she went over to check the text and silence the phone.

When her eyes finally focused on the message, Alexis felt chills collecting at the nape of her neck. She became so tense that she felt paralyzed as she felt all the blood drain from her face. Alexis heard her door open and someone walk in, but she didn't move. Her eyes remained focus on the text message on the screen.

"Lex? Are you ok?" Alexis recognized the voice and knew it was Sharonda, but she couldn't make out exactly what she was saying. She felt Sharonda walked over to her and try to touch her, but she jerked away quickly. Alexis looked up and stared her in the face as if she were a stranger.

"Lex? It's me! What's going....Oh my God! Did you just pee on yourself?" Mortified, Alexis followed Sharonda's stare and looked down at her own legs. While she stared down at the wet trail streaming down from between her legs, she began to feel herself growing faint.

"I'm going to call Ms. Juice!" As she watched Sharonda walk out of the room, Alexis realized that she still had a death grip on her cell phone. She let her eyes fall back to the message. It was only two words, but those two words made her feel sick to her stomach. Almost to the point of throwing up.

Sorry, Lex.

"What the fuck was that about, Lex? Damn, girl! I thought I was gonna have to take you to the hospital or something!" Sharonda said smacking on her gum. Alexis sipped on her glass of water silently. She didn't want to explain the text message to Sharonda, but she had a feeling that it would not be as easy as she wished to avoid the topic.

Ms. Juice had told her that she was not in the right to state to work for the day, so she promptly ordered Sharonda to help her take a bath and leave. The John had not been happy about being dumped off on his second favorite girl in the house when he had specifically requested Alexis, but Alexis knew he would get over it and be back soon. After Sharonda helped her clean up, she suggested they go over to a pizza spot downtown and grab something to eat. Alexis wanted to have some fresh air, so they had decided to eat outside.

"I'm aight, Ronda." Alexis said stuffing her mouth full of her pepperoni and mushroom pizza. She grabbed a napkin to wipe the grease off her fingers before smoothing out her red silk dress. She crossed her legs and tapped her gold Louboutins on one of the legs of the table in an effort to calm herself down. She still felt sick to her stomach about the text message.

Why the hell would he contact me? I don't give a fuck about no damn apology! Alexis could feel the anxiety building inside of her. Her eyes darted around the area. She had the creepy feeling that she was being watched. Alexis took a deep breath and tried to calm herself.

"Naw, bitch. What was with that message? I saw you gripping up on that phone. What was that about?" Sharonda grabbed her Coke and started sucking loudly on the straw. Alexis watched her for a minute. She could understand why Sharonda had so many dedicated clients. Homegirl was putting the work down on that straw.

"Someone contacted me. Someone I hadn't expected to hear from again." Alexis said quietly. She ducked her head in shame and then caught herself. She lifted her head back up, cleared her throat and look Sharonda right in the eye. She could tell from Sharonda's stare that she knew exactly who she was referring to.

"Oh. Well, what did this person text you?"

Shit. I knew she wouldn't just drop the subject.

"He said he was sorry." Alexis whispered. She felt her throat closing up as she thought about it. Beads of sweat popped up around her hairline. She brushed them away quickly and tried to regain her composure.

"Fuck that nigga." Sharonda said before grabbing another slice of pizza and stuffing over half of it down her throat.

Got damn, this bitch got skills!

"That's right." Alexis said sitting up straight in her seat. "Fuck 'em." Soon as she said it, her phone chirped again. Alexis looked over at the text and felt the fear set in again.

"What?" Sharonda asked. Alexis pushed her phone over to her so that she could see the text.

I'm in Atlanta. I want to apologize to you in person so you know I mean it. I'm sorry. Sharonda grabbed the phone and pressed a few buttons.

"Text deleted. Ignore that nigga. You can't dwell on this shit. You gotta move on." Alexis nodded her head. It made sense, but she wasn't sure how she was supposed to be able to do that.

"So what you gonna do about Ms. Juice?" Sharonda asked throwing down the crust of her pizza.

"What do you mean?" Alexis asked. She knew that Sharonda couldn't have been asking about what she had discussed earlier with Ms. Juice. How could she know that already?

"You know...about her wanting you to start fucking the clients. She got some nerve, don't she?" Sharonda kept slurping up her soda as if it wasn't anything that she just happened to know information that Alexis hadn't even discussed with her yet.

"Uh...well, I told her no." Alexis said uneasily.

"She ain't going for that shit. So what are you going to do? She ain't playin'! She *will* kick your ass out."

"Well, then I guess she will have to kick my ass out." Alexis said before biting off more of her pizza. Sharonda looked at her hard for a minute. Much like the same way that she had looked at her that day at the clinic. Alexis tried to avoid her stare. Finally Sharonda shrugged her shoulders and pulled off another slice of pizza from the pie.

"Ok, fine. Hope that works for you." She said chomping away at her slice.

"So do I." Alexis responded.

So do I.

"SO WHERE YOU BEEN?" MARC ASKED AS HE BIT OFF A PIECE OF A GREEN apple that he was holding. He eyed her with suspicion as he chewed. In what appeared to be an effort to appear menacing, he seemed to forget to close his mouth while chewing and Alexis flinched from the smacking sound that he was making.

"Hanging out with a friend, Marc. That's all." Alexis said walking around him to the refrigerator. She opened it up and grabbed out a ginger ale. She needed something to settle her stomach. She was doing better, but every time she thought about Dexter texting her, she felt like throwing up.

"You hang out with a friend every single day now? Why can't you stay home anymore?" Alexis turned around so fast that she almost continued spinning to make a full 360 degree turn.

"Excuse me? So I'm supposed to stay my ass in the house all day? Your ass is usually out of town on *business* so what's the difference? Isn't it bout that time for you to get up out of here and out of my shit anyways? Damn!" Alexis looked at Marc and watched his expression change. He looked like he was struggling to find the words to respond. "You got something to say, Marc?"

"Lexi, I didn't mean it like that. All I'm saying is that you've been gone a lot. I would just like to know why. Especially with what happened...." Marc allowed his voice to trail off.

"This isn't about that shit. Now I already said drop it, so drop it!" Alexis said as she walked in close to his face. She expected Marc to back down if she became confrontational. He normally did so that he could avoid a fight or upsetting her.

"I'm not dropping shit. I've given you time and now you need to speak. So tell me what the fuck happened and who did it! Now, Alexis." Marc walked in closer to her. He stood up straight and frowned up his face. Although Alexis was sure that he'd never hurt her, something about his stance seemed to make her feel slightly threatened. But she refused to back down, so she held her position and threw him a return glare.

"I just told you this isn't about that shit. Now get the fuck out of my face." Alexis jumped when Marc grabbed her by the wrist.

"We are going to talk about what happened, Alexis. I know you were raped. Who did it? Do you know?" Marc said roughly. Alexis snatched her arm away from him and pushed him back. She was much smaller than him, so he barely moved, but it still shocked him. The surprised look on Marc's face almost made her laugh. But she was too pissed off to laugh about anything at the moment.

"Don't ever grab me like that again! Now leave me the hell alone or else." Alexis warned as she walked pass him and climbed up the stairs. She heard a loud noise and resisted the urge to turn around and make sure that Marc was ok. Two seconds later she realized she didn't really care either way.

He can have that temper tantrum on his own.

KAYLEN

$\mathcal{K}$aylen sighed out loud. All this studying was making her eyes tired. She couldn't really focus on the material anyways. Everything she read was important, but she couldn't think about anything but Caleb. Kaylen slammed her book closed and opened her laptop to check her bank account. She had been resisting the urge to fall back into her previous forms of earning money, but it was starting to look like she needed to give a few people a call. Although she hated Dom and they always found something to bicker about whenever they ran into each other, she knew that he was someone who Levi had trusted when they were younger and she could possibly use his assistance. She picked up her phone to dial the last number that she'd had for Dom, but was interrupted when she heard a car door slam shut in front of her townhouse.

Tiny ran over and began barking and clawing at the front door. Shortly after, she heard her doorbell ring. Kaylen sat her laptop to the side and started walking towards the door. She peeked through the peep hole and saw it was a guy with a UPS uniform on. Kaylen opened the door quickly.

"Hi, I have a package for Kaylen Washington." The man said as he jabbed on the pad he was holding. When he finally took a minute to look up at Kaylen, his eyes lingered for a minute and he smiled. Kaylen decided to flirt a little and smiled back.

"I'm Kaylen." She responded, still smiling. The man handed over the tablet for her to sign her signature and he continued to watch her as she took her time signing.

"Well, here you are. Have a great day." The man said handing over her package.

"I will. Just make sure you do the same." Kaylen winked. The man smiled even wider and turned to head back to his car.

Kaylen closed the door behind her and looked down at the box. It had no return address on the outside.

"Hmmm...ok, who is this from?" Kaylen said as she opened it up. Inside, there was a smaller box that was gift wrapped. On top of it was a card. Kaylen grabbed the card first and opened it.

I have missed you. Hope you are doing well. Just wanted to send you a little something to celebrate your birthday. Hope it is better this year around. Love, Zo.

Kaylen's heart stopped and she read the card about three more times before placing it down on the table. She hadn't heard from Zo in months and now, here he was. Sending her something for her birthday. A birthday that she had totally forgot about, but somehow he remembered.

"How in the world did he know my birthday was coming up?" Kaylen asked herself out loud. He had no way of knowing, but Zo always seemed to have insight into things for some reason. Kaylen grabbed the big rectangular box and pulled the wrapping paper off of it, and then she looked at the box. The top of the box read Dolce & Gabbana. Kaylen pulled the top off the box and pulled out the prettiest gold sequined dress that she had ever seen.

"Oh my God..." she said breathlessly. She couldn't have picked out a better dress if she had been in the store herself. A small piece of paper fell out of the dress as she pulled it out of the box. Kaylen picked it up and read the words.

I would love to see you in this for your big day. Hope you like the shoes.

"Shoes?" Kaylen said pulling up the bottom part of the rectangular box. Underneath was another box that read Dolce & Gabbana.

Wow...he has amazing taste. Kaylen pulled the top off and saw gold stilettos to match the dress. She definitely was impressed and couldn't wait to wear them. Kaylen grabbed her cell phone and thumbed through her contact list to the number that she had been staring at nearly every day for the past five months, but had been too afraid to call. She still was afraid to call, so she decided to send a quick text.

Got the package.

"No...no...that's sounds dumb." Kaylen erased the text.

Got the gift. I love it. Thanks so much.

"Should I send it?" Kaylen asked herself. She looked back over at the card. "Oh, yeah..."

I've missed you, too. She sent the text and then grabbed the dress and shoes so that she could take it to her room. Before she left the table, she heard her cell phone chime. She placed the boxes back down and checked her phone.

Glad you loved it. Where will you be celebrating your birthday? Kaylen bit her lip as she thought for a second. She hadn't had a chance to plan anything because she had totally forgotten about it. She knew she wanted to go out with Alexis and Jazmyn, but she hadn't even thought pass that.

I think I'm just going to hit up Rain with Lexi and Jaz. Want to come? Kaylen started biting her nails as she waited for Zo's response.

Sure. Kaylen starred at the word for about five minutes before placing the phone down on the table. She looked back at the dress and the shoes and then started towards the room to put them up until her birthday. She made a mental note to contact Nesha to get her hair done the day before.

❦

"HELLO? KAY?"

"Caleb, why do you sound out of breath? What were you doing?" Kaylen asked. She wasn't even trying to disguise the attitude in her voice. She was pissed off. Caleb was at a conference so in her mind, he had no reason to sound out of breath. There was nothing he should have been doing at the conference that would have caused him to be breathing hard. Except...

"I'm not out of breath, Kay. Or at least I hope not. I just walked up a few flights of stairs rather than taking the elevator. If I'm out of breath from that, then I need to get in better shape." Caleb chuckled, but Kaylen didn't see a damn thing funny.

He must think I'm dumb.

"Well, what are you planning on doing tonight, Caleb? The conference doesn't start until tomorrow, right?" Kaylen looked at the clock on her nightstand as she rolled over on her bed. It was almost 7 o'clock at night in LA. The night was still young.

"I think I need to grab something to eat. I'm pretty hungry. Then, I may just call it a night. I need to look over some new developments in the field before the conference starts tomorrow. Although it's meant to be a learning process, you know how doctors can be when they think you should have already heard about something."

"Yes, you're right." Caleb's nervousness made her smile. His need to prove himself is something that she had not known about him in the past, but it was an insecurity that she had begun to like about him. He was much younger than many other physicians that he worked with, so he always felt the need to go the extra mile to prove that he was just as good a professor as they were.

"Do you have any plans for the night? I know it's another night alone, are you holding up ok?" Kaylen sucked in a breath as she thought about what he said. She hadn't even thought about the fact that she had not really stayed the night by herself since the night Salem died. She had called Caleb after Zo left and he'd been with her every day since...either at her place or his. She didn't have an issue last night, but she'd been up studying so it didn't really make a difference. She thought about how the last time she fell asleep alone, she woke up and Salem was in her house, threatening to kill her.

"I think I will be fine. Where are you going for dinner?" Kaylen asked as she walked out of her room to go check her lock on the front and back doors.

"There is a restaurant on the first floor of the hotel. I think I may just check it out."

"Alone?" As soon as Kaylen said it, she regretted it but it was too late.

"Yes, alone." Caleb said in an aggravated tone. "Hold on, someone is at the door." Kaylen heard some fumbling around and she assumed that Caleb had laid the phone down somewhere. Kaylen pressed her ear close to the phone so that she could hear.

"Hi, Caleb! I heard you were here at this conference, how are you?" Kaylen face turned to a frown as she listened.

That better not be Nikki!

"Uh...hey...I'm well. You know, this is not the best time. Can I call you later?" Kaylen scrunched up her face.

What does he need to call her later for?

"Sure! Well, actually I was just wondering if you wanted to go down with me for something to eat."

"Um...yeah, Shaun. You know what? Can you hold on a minute?"

Shaun? Who the hell is Shaun? Seconds later, Kaylen heard some more scuffling on the line.

"Kay, hey baby, I'm about to go with a colleague to dinner. I will give you a call later on tonight." It took a minute for Kaylen to work up a response.

"Uh....I love you, Caleb." Kaylen said. She figured she would save the yelling for later and at least make sure that Shaun heard him say those three words to her before he marched off to have dinner with her and play footsies under the table.

"Yeah, me too. Bye!" Kaylen's mouth fell open as she pulled the phone away from her ear and looked at it. Those were definitely not the three words she was looking for.

"Who is Shaun?" Kaylen said to herself after the line went dead. Caleb had spoken to her in the past about women. So many that she couldn't count, but the name Shaun didn't ring a bell.

"This better not be a brand new bitch!" Kaylen huffed as Tiny nudged her leg out of concern. Kaylen looked back at her phone and contemplated texting Zo. There was no better way to get over being upset with one man than to text your fallback nigga. After two seconds of thinking about it, she gave in to the temptation.

I'm curious. How much do you miss me? Kaylen hurried and sent the text before she lost all nerve. About a minute later her phone beeped.

Enough to want to see you. Kaylen couldn't suppress the huge grin that came to her face.

What happened to what's her face? Zo had been "dating" some girl the last time she saw him. She wasn't sure what happened to ole girl, but she was curious.

What happened to what's his face? Zo responded back.

"Damn! How does he know about Caleb?" Kaylen asked herself.

How do you know about him? She figured the best way to find out was to ask directly.

I make it my business to keep up with you. Kaylen smiled even wider. She sat looking at the text for a minute.

"What should I say back?" Kaylen asked out loud as she flopped down backwards onto her bed. She placed one leg on top of the knee of the other and stared at the screen of her phone. She felt like she was back in high school again trying to figure out what she should say to her crush.

So when can I see you? Zo's message popped on her screen before Kaylen even had a chance to respond to his last one. She felt a tingling sensation in her stomach as she tried to think about how to answer his question. She didn't want to seem too anxious, but she didn't want to make it seem like she didn't want to see him either.

How about tomorrow night? Kaylen started to bite her nails as she waited for a response.

I will bring Chinese.

"My favorite thing to eat. Wow, he really does keep up with me." Kaylen said as she laid the phone on the bed. Part of her wanted to feel a little guilty for meeting with Zo when Caleb was out of town. Then again, he was having dinner with Shaun at that exact moment, so she brushed the guilt off and went back to studying.

JAZMYN

*C*rimson.

She had been here. She probably was still here. She probably had been watching everything happen since Jazmyn had walked away from the taxi. Suddenly Jazmyn heard knocking on the windshield and she nearly jumped straight through the roof of the car.

"Jaz?" Jazmyn turned in the direction of the voice and saw Kingston looking through the window at her. In his arms, he was balancing LaShea who was smiling widely as she looked at Jazmyn with drool falling from the sides of her lop-sided grin. Jazmyn opened the car door and stepped out with Kingston assisting her by offering his other arm.

"I see you have already had a chance to check out the new car!" Kingston said with a big smile.

"Uh...yes. Wait, you know about this?" Jazmyn stammered. She was unsure how much Kingston knew and did not want to give him any additional information.

"Yeah...your business partner came by. A woman. She said that you received a promotion or something and they bought you a new car! Congratulations, baby! So when can we stop by and see the new job?" Kingston asked grinning from ear to ear. More questions.

Never.

"Um...did she say anything else? My business partner..." Jazmyn said walking into the house.

"No, she just said that was your new car. Hey...where is your old one? How did you get home?" Kingston asked looking back out the window to the street.

"How are you, babygirl?" Jazmyn asked ignoring Kingston's question. She pulled LaShea from Kingston's arms and hugged her close as the baby giggled happily. It hadn't taken Jazmyn long to get over her sins. She had murdered Shanice, for something that wasn't really her fault in the beginning. She couldn't fault Shanice for being upset that her husband was sleeping around with another woman, even if she could blame her for being such a bitch about it. Jazmyn would have sliced Kingston from ear to ear if he had been cheating on her while she was pregnant with his baby. But in the end, Shanice decided to be grimy with the blackmail and she wrote a check that her ass couldn't cash. Plus the baby wasn't even Kingston's, so she was doing her own thing on the side also. She was a hypocrite and was fucking with the wrong people which eventually led to her death.

After Shanice was finished and Jazmyn had slipped out the window of LaShea's bedroom, Jazmyn had been driving home when Kingston called her. She had no idea what to say to him. What do you say to a man after you just killed his pregnant wife and cut the baby out of her stomach?

"Yes?" Jazmyn had answered the phone quietly and ridden with guilt. Usually when she completed missions for Crimson and Dom, she had no connections whatsoever with the person, so she just thought about as a job...something that needed to be done. This time she felt guilty because although she hated Kingston for having a wife, the fact is that he did have a wife and he had at one point loved her. Maybe even still did. Jazmyn felt guilty knowing that she had left him to discover tragic news once he returned home.

"Baby...Jaz, thanks for answering my call." Kingston sounded defeated, sad and tired.

Has someone already told him about Shanice? No...there is no way. I just left there!

"Kingston? Are you ok?" Jazmyn asked as she turned into her parking space in front of her condo.

"Yes...baby, I need you. I left Shanice. I'm done with her. She told me all about how she has been cheating for over a year. I don't want her anymore. I want to be with you."

"Where are you?" Jazmyn asked. She had expected him to be at the gym, but it didn't sound like that's where he was.

"At *Twelve*, in our room. I'm going to stay here until I figure shit out. Can you come here with me?" Jazmyn laid her head down on her steering wheel. She knew her answer should have been no, but she didn't want him to be alone. Especially when she knew what lay in store for him. His whole life was about to change and he didn't even know it. He would be getting a call any minute now after the police arrived on the scene.

"I'm on my way." Jazmyn said placing her car into reverse.

"I can't wait to see you. I need you. I will let them know downstairs that you are on your way." Kingston said. He was already beginning to sound better. Jazmyn loved the way his entire mood changed at the possibility of seeing her.

"Kingston...did Shanice tell you who she was cheating with?" Jazmyn wanted to know what would happen to the baby that she had allowed to live. She hadn't really thought the details out before. She didn't even know what would happen to the little girl now that her mother was dead.

"No, she just told me it was some guy she had been messing with for a while. I don't really care. I just know I'm done with her. I've been done with her."

"I will see you in about fifteen." Jazmyn said disconnecting the call.

"Damn! What the hell was I thinking letting that baby live?" Jazmyn had yelled to herself. In her opinion, she may have just opened up another can of problems that she would have to deal with at some other time.

Now it was months later and Jazmyn was holding the baby girl in her arms. She had never wanted to be a mother to LaShea, but when she and Kingston moved in together, she assumed that role out of guilt more than anything. She knew how it was growing up without her father. She had taken this girl's mother from her and she felt a responsibility to...do what? Not raise her, but somehow that's what Kingston had expected and that was what she was helping him do.

Jazmyn handed LaShea back to Kingston and walked into the kitchen.

"Where are we ordering from for dinner tonight?" Jazmyn asked. Cooking was not her thing. She'd heard Kaylen talking to her old friend Levi a lot in the past about how well she cooked, but she'd never taken the time to ask Kaylen to teach her. She probably never would either. Jazmyn had no desire to learn how to prepare a meal when takeout was readily available and probably tasted a dozen times better.

"Chinese?" Kingston asked placing LaShea inside of her playpen.

"Sure, I will call."

"Wow, the takeout got here pretty fast this time." Kingston said looking down at his watch. LaShea was playing with blue, purple and white blocks at his feet.

"You heard a knock at the door?" Jazmyn asked him. As soon as the last word left her mouth, the doorbell rang.

"No, I heard a car pull up. But you heard that doorbell just now, right?" Kingston joked winking at her.

"Yes, Kingston. I'm not hard of hearing." Jazmyn laughed rolling her eyes as she went to answer the door. Once she pulled the door open, she was startled to see that it wasn't a delivery man standing at the door at all. Instead it was a tall, caramel-colored, well dressed man with a black sweater and nice blue jeans. Jazmyn paused for a second wondering if she knew him.

This isn't someone I dated, is it? Jazmyn asked herself as she went through her Rolodex of men in her mind.

"Hi, can I help you?" Kingston said from behind her. Apparently he thought he should step in since Jazmyn had not yet opened her mouth.

"Yes, are you Kingston?" the man asked as he turned his attention from Jazmyn to where Kingston stood. Jazmyn stepped back a little out of the doorway to allow Kingston to get closer. LaShea scrawled over to where they were standing and began pulled at Kingston's pants leg. The man looked down at LaShea and a small smile teased the edge of his lips.

"Yes, I'm Kingston. Who are you?" Kingston asked as he bent down to pick up LaShea. She cooed happily as she lay against his chest.

"My name is Trey Anderson. I need to speak to you for a minute if you don't mind." The man asked, his eyes still rested on LaShea.

"Ok, then. You can come inside." Shocked, Jazmyn turned quickly to shoot a glance at Kingston. *You can tell black folks that were raised in the suburbs. You do not just invite strangers into your damn house!* Jazmyn thought as she watched Kingston lead Trey into the family room. She followed behind and took a seat. Although Trey looked harmless, she knew from her work experience that you should never trust appearance. They are seldom what they seem.

"Ok, so how can I help you?" Kingston asked as he placed LaShea down on the floor so that she could continue playing with her blocks. Trey sat down across from him and continued looking at the baby. Jazmyn wrinkled up her nose as she watched him.

"You like babies or something?" Jazmyn asked him.

I may need to go grab my knife for this perverted motherfucker.

"Uh...well, that's what I need to speak to you about, Kingston." Trey said adjusting his gaze and looking at Kingston. He paused and looked down while fumbling with his fingers.

"Yes?" Kingston said looking at Trey, now with suspicion. He picked LaShea up and placed her in his lap out of caution. Jazmyn squinted at him.

No time to get cautious now. That's why you don't just let anyone inside your damn house! Jazmyn thought as she turned back to look at Trey. Trey cleared his throat and began to speak.

"Well, about two years ago I met Shanice and we started dating." Trey cleared his throat again. He looked up at Kingston and then back down to his hands. Jazmyn cleared her throat and sat up straight in her seat.

Oh my God! I know this is not who I think this is. Jazmyn thought to herself. She looked over to Kingston and tried to read his expression. Kingston's light complexion was even lighter than normal and it looked like all the blood drained from his face as he began to realize who this man was.

"Well, anyways...she told me that she wasn't involved with anyone. I didn't think she was when we started sleeping...uh...when we started being intimate." Trey sighed and looked up briefly at Kingston who was gripping LaShea so tightly that she began wiggling in lap. "Anyways, when she told me she was pregnant, she broke up with me. She told me that the baby was yours and she was getting back with you." Trey paused again and looked at Kingston who seemed to be in a trance. He wasn't saying anything at all, but he was looking at Trey with such anger that it made Jazmyn adjust nervously in her seat.

"Listen, Kingston, I really had no idea that she was married until she told me she was pregnant. She always told me that her life was complicated....I never questioned why she couldn't spend the night or why she never called me at certain times. It just never seemed important to me at the time. I just loved being able to share time with her." Trey shrugged and looked at Kingston as if he were waiting for a response.

"What are you doing here?" Kingston said slowly. Jazmyn looked at him and saw that he no longer appeared angry. His shoulders were slouched down and his eyes were sad. He knew what Trey was doing here. And in a few minutes, his thoughts would be confirmed.

"I'm here because...well, I found out what happened to Shanice. I recently tried to contact her through some mutual friends of ours and I found out that she was murdered by some gang member or drug dealer or something. Wow, I just never would have thought..." Jazmyn noticed that Trey's eyes had filled up with tears. She almost felt sorry for him, but then she looked at Kingston and noticed that his eyes had tears in them as well. She knew Kingston enough to know that he would never let them fall, but he was struggling with his emotions at the moment and it bothered her.

"I was also told that she had a paternity test done on the baby and that she is not yours. So, I wanted to come speak to you about my... daughter. I want my daughter. I want her to come live with me." Trey straightened up in his chair as he finished and looked at Kingston. Kingston continued staring back at the man while holding LaShea, who was beginning to whine as she continued squirming for freedom in his lap.

Jazmyn tried to keep her jaw from falling to the floor. She was not expecting this to happen. She had a feeling that Trey's visit wasn't going to end well once he started his story, but she wasn't prepared for him to ask for the baby permanently. Maybe visitation or something...but, damn! Could he even get her back? The lawyer in her kicked in.

"Kingston is LaShea's legal father. Him and Shanice were married when she was conceived." Jazmyn responded as she tried to gather her thoughts together. She looked over at Kingston who had not moved. LaShea began whining louder and it finally grabbed his attention. He placed her back on the floor and she began happily playing with her toys once more.

"I know," Trey responded. "And I'm ready to take this through the courts. She is...*if* she is my daughter, I want her to live with me." Jazmyn stood up from her seat and grabbed the notepad and pencil that they kept on the coffee table in the living room.

"Write your name and number on this sheet of paper." Trey obeyed and then handed the pad back to her.

"It's time to go. We will keep in touch." Jazmyn said standing over Trey. She crossed her arms in front of her and waited for him to move. "It's time to go." She repeated. Trey shrugged and stood up from his seat. He looked at LaShea before walking towards the door.

"I will be hiring an attorney tomorrow. I want to move fast on this. I have always wanted kids, and I will have my daughter living with me." Trey said as Jazmyn opened the door. She waited for him to walk out before slamming the door behind him. Jazmyn turned around and saw Kingston sitting with his head in his hands. LaShea had pulled herself up so that she was standing and resting one hand on his legs to steady herself; her other hand was patting Kingston on the back of the head as if to ask what was wrong with him. Jazmyn sighed heavily. This was a situation that she had created because she hadn't tied up her lose ends. Crimson had always told her about that.

Somehow I gotta handle this shit.

ALEXIS

"*L*exi, you almost ready?" Marc called from down the stairs. Alexis rolled her eyes and ignored him. In her mind, he should have been happy that she was going on this date at all after what had happened the other night. She really did not feel like traipsing around Atlanta pretending to be the perfect couple. However, she didn't feel like being holed up in the house either.

Alexis picked up her eye shadow and dabbed a little color onto her eyelids before throwing it back down on the bathroom counter. She wasn't in the mood for much primping at the moment. She looked at herself in the mirror. Although she was still beautiful according to normal standards, she could see a difference about her. She was hardened. There used to be a happiness about her. But that was long gone.

The crazy thing is that Alexis wasn't sure that she missed that side of her. That was the side of her that was in denial about how things really were. She was innocent and lived as if her upper class problems with her husband were the worst things that could happen to anyone. She had friends that thought they knew her, but did they really? If your friends don't know your biggest, most horrible secrets...are they really your friends at all?

Alexis ran her fingers through her hair before turning around and walking out of the master bathroom. She paused in her room only long enough to grab her purse from off of her reading chair and walked out of the room. Marc was downstairs looking up at her as she walked down the stairs. She sucked in a breath and tried to prepare herself mentally for a night out on the town with her husband. She would rather have been anywhere else in the world at that moment.

"You look nice, Alexis." Marc said as he watched her walk down the stairs. Alexis didn't bother answering, she just nodded her head slightly and Marc seemed satisfied with her response.

"Alright, let's get going. We are already going to be a little late for our reservation." Marc said grabbing her hand. Alexis allowed him to hold it, but she still made it go limp. Marc responded by clutching on tighter. He led her out of the house, locked the door, then he walked with her to the passenger side of their black Mercedes-Benz ML63 and opened the door for her to get in. Alexis released his hand and jumped into her side of the SUV without a second thought.

The entire ride to the restaurant Marc tried to make small talk and Alexis ignored him. It really didn't seem worth her time to even speak to him when she was so upset. It wouldn't lead to anything but arguing anyways. Unfortunately, she had not been able to get to Ms. Juice's establishment that day to settle her anger. Alexis knew that her dedicated clients were growing impatient with her not being available during their regularly scheduled appointment.

Shit, I'm pissed about it too, Alexis said as she glanced over at Marc from the side of her eye. It was his fault that she hadn't been able to make it. After their argument the night before, he made sure to sit around the house and watch her all morning. Alexis knew he was waiting for her to get ready to leave so that he could bitch about it. She was so annoyed with him that she ended up staying in the room all day to avoid him.

"So...I'm going to start back going to work sometime next week again. If you wanna go, then..." At the perfect second, Alexis' phone started ringing. She hurriedly reached down into her gold Michael Kors clutch and grabbed her phone.

"Hold on, Marc. It's Duchess." Alexis said as she pressed the 'answer' button before placing the phone to her ear. Normally, she wasn't so excited when Duchess called, but she was eager to take the call this time in order to avoid conversation with Marc.

"Hi, Duchess."

"Countess! What has been going on with you? I have not heard from you in weeks." Duchess was speaking fast and she sounded a little distracted. That wasn't really anything new. She was the queen of balancing multiple things at one time and only giving her children a corner of her attention.

"I've been a little busy, that's all. How's Vanessa? She still living with you guys?" Alexis tried to change the subject because she did not want to get into why she hadn't been visiting or really speaking to either of her parents on a regular basis. As far as she knew, Vanessa had kept her secret and hadn't told anyone besides Marc about the rape. She promised not to tell anyone about the baby at all, and Alexis wanted to keep things as they were.

"Yeah, she's here." Duchess said drily. Alexis could visualize the huge eye roll that accompanied Duchess' much less than excited response.

"What is the problem?" Alexis asked as she leaned her head on the window and listened. She noticed that Marc was sighing heavily, but she continued to ignore him.

"Well, you know the issues she's been having with Sasha, right?" Duchess paused as she waited for Alexis to respond.

"No, she never did tell me everything about that. What happened?" Alexis wrinkled her brow as she listened. If she knew her sister like she thought she did, whatever was going on with Vanessa was about to be juicy. Alexis needed a distraction in her life.

"That girl, Sasha, that she was staying with. Something happened between Vanessa and her boyfriend. She didn't really get into it with me, but it was bad enough to make Vanessa decide to leave her condo. The condo that your father and I are still paying for, I might add." Alexis groaned out loud. She needed to speak with her sister. She couldn't go around trying to bed everyone's man. She was looking for love in all the wrong places.

"I see. Well, I have to go, Duchess. I will talk to you later on." Alexis said looking out the window. They had made it to their destination and valet was waiting for them to step out of the car. Alexis pressed the "end" button on the phone and looked over at Marc who was staring hard at her.

"You ready now?" He asked. She could tell he was annoyed.

"Hold on a minute." Alexis said and pulled down the mirror. She reached into her bag and pulled out her lip gloss. She didn't need to reapply it, but Marc's attitude was getting on her nerves. He sighed loudly as he watched and Alexis tried to hide her smirk.

"I'm ready now." She said as she tossed the lip gloss into her bag and signaled to the valet to come over and open her door. She stepped out of the car and all eyes immediately went to her. She was wearing a short and snug gold, sparkly dress. It hugged all her curves just the right way. It wasn't normally something that she would wear on a date out with her husband, but tonight she wanted to feel powerful and sexy so this was the obvious choice.

"Hi, we have reservations for two under Marc Soriano." The hostess' eyes lit up when she saw Marc and Alexis laughed inside.

If she only knew what I had to put up with being with him.

"Sure, this is Mindy. She will show you to your table." She pointed to a young and busty brunette with a wide smile.

"Right this way!" Mindy said, ushering them to follow her with her hand. Alexis fought the urge to shake her head at the extreme thirst being thrown at Marc as the woman swished her hips from side to side while leading them to their table. Marc grabbed Alexis hand and led her to where they were to be seated.

"Here is your table! Is this ok for you?" Alexis was going to object and state that she would rather sit at a booth, but she realized that the woman wasn't even speaking to her. She hadn't bothered to acknowledge her presence at all. Attitude set in immediately and she snatched her hand away from Marc then folded her arms across her chest.

"Actually...." Alexis started.

"This table will be just fine." Marc jumped in. "Thank you!" Mindy winked and walked away, swishing even harder than before. Marc pulled out a chair for Alexis and she gave him a hard look.

"I would have rathered a booth." Alexis said as she sat down in the chair. Marc ignored her as he pushed her in under the table and walked over to sit in his own chair.

"Did you hear me?" Alexis repeated. Marc nodded his head and then picked up a menu.

"Alexis, let's try to make this a good night, ok?" Marc mumbled. Alexis groaned and looked around the restaurant. It was pretty crowded at the time. *Frank Ski's Restaurant Lounge* was a very nice establishment in Midtown. Alexis had only been there once with Kaylen and Jazmyn, but she didn't remember it because she had been pretty drunk that night. Thinking about it made her laugh inside. The entire night she was throwing back drinks and her girls kept them coming. She missed them.

Just at that moment, Alexis saw Vanessa walk into the restaurant with a very handsome man. He had a dark chocolate complexion with a very low-cut and was easily the best dressed in the restaurant, although Marc had always easily took that prize. He was walking and his hand was nestled comfortably on her lower back, leading her through the restaurant to their table. Vanessa looked happy, but something was slightly off. She seemed a little sad as well...Alexis became interested immediately.

"Marc, I just saw Vanessa walk in. I will be back. I want to say 'hello'." Alexis said as she rose from her chair. She didn't even wait for Marc's response, but it didn't seem like he was poised to give one anyways. Alexis walked slowly over to where Vanessa sat and she observed the interaction. The man seemed to be overly excited about having Vanessa as his date. His body language said it all. They were sitting in the lounge seating area, where there were plush sofas rather than booths or chairs. He had sat down so him and Vanessa where on one of the sofas and he was leaning so closely into her that he was almost part of her outfit. Although Vanessa appeared interested and delighted with his presence, Alexis knew her sister enough to know she was not having the time of her life and would rather be some-where else.

"Vanessa?" Alexis said once she was at the table. Vanessa's eyes shot up in surprise when she saw her sister standing before her. Her date looked at Alexis with interest.

"Lexi! Hey, what are you doing here?" Vanessa asked as if it were a crime for Alexis to be out of the house. She surveyed Alexis' outfit quickly and, although she obviously approved of her fashion choice, she was definitely surprised to see Alexis wearing it.

"Marc and I are at dinner." Vanessa's eyes drooped down as soon as Alexis mentioned Marc. Apparently, she was still feeling guilty.

"Hi...well I'm Denzo." The man leaned stood up and held his hand out for Alexis. She reached out and allowed him to shake hers. He seemed to be very polite, handsome, extremely well-dressed so he had to have some kind of a bank account. What was the problem?

"Nice to meet you. I'm Vanessa's sister."

"Sister?" Denzo asked. Vanessa looked uneasy and he turned to give her a confused look.

Obviously she hasn't even bothered to tell him anything about the family yet.

"Uh...Vanessa, can I speak to you for a minute?" Vanessa nodded and slid out from under the table. She followed Alexis to a large empty space near the front of the restaurant. Alexis turned to see what Marc was doing and noticed that he was watching with an annoyed look on his face. She shrugged and turned towards Vanessa.

"So, who is this guy and why do you look sick in the face?" Alexis asked. Vanessa looked flawless as usual. She had let her hair grow out and had it in a cute style where her curly tresses fell on one side of her head. She had on long diamond earrings and they complimented the sparkle in her short-sleeved top that was cropped short enough to show off her washboard abs. She had on grey pleated pants and sparkly white stilettos that were to die for. The only thing wrong was the pouty expression that she had plastered on her face.

"I'm trying to date." Vanessa mumbled. This was new. Alexis had never known Vanessa to have a boyfriend in her life. Well...there was this one guy that she dated in high school, but she was so secretive about the relationship that it couldn't have been all that serious.

"Well, he looks like a good start. Why do you look so sick about it?" Alexis asked as she glance back over at Denzo. He did seem to be a good start if Vanessa was looking to actually settle her ass down in a relationship and stop using men for only sex.

"I don't think I'm ready. I don't think I will ever fall in love again after Ty." Alexis jerked her head back towards Vanessa and stared at her with confusion.

"Who is Ty? Wait.....fall in love? When did you fall in love with someone?" She had never heard her sister mention being in a serious relationship with anyone. The name Ty did sound familiar though.

Wait...was Ty that guy that she dated in high school? In love....how out of the loop was I?

"Hey! It's you!" Alexis was jarred out of her own thoughts when she heard the loud voice. It was one she recognized, but this was not the place that she had expected to hear it.

"I've been trying to see you. Are you not working at Ms. Juice's joint anymore?" Alexis looked in horror at one of the Johns that frequented Ms. Juice's place to spend time with her. Her mouth fell open and she just stared silently. She had never thought about what would happen if she ever saw one of them in public.

"I'm sorry...do you know her?" Vanessa said. She was looking back and forth between the man and Alexis as she tried to figure out what was going on.

"Yes, I do. And she has been wasting a lot of my money. You do know that bitch charges us even if we don't do anything, right? She charges me monthly!" The man spat at Alexis. Alexis finally closed her open mouth and squinted at him. She was utterly surprised. At Ms. Juice's this man acted like a little mouse, scared to speak and do anything other than what she'd asked him to do. Now he was acting as if he ran shit.

"Is there a problem here?" Alexis cursed under her breath when she heard Marc's voice.

Why couldn't he just stay his ass at the table? Damn!

"Yes! Do you know this b..." The man started.

"Yes, there is is a problem, Marc. I don't know him...I th...I think he has me...uh, confused with someone else." Alexis stammered as she backed away from the man and towards Marc.

"What?! I don't have a thing confused!" The man yelled. Patrons of the restaurant were starting to stare and Alexis saw the manager heading their way.

"I think you need to leave." Vanessa said to the man. She had a deep frown on her face and she spoke very sternly to the man, but it didn't make a difference. He was angry.

"Is there a problem?" The manager asked as he looked from person to person. Long pause.

"You know what? No, there is no problem. I thought I knew her, but, actually, I don't." The man said as he glared down at Alexis.

Marc eyed the man suspiciously and looked back at his wife. Alexis tried to avoid his eyes but he was staring at her with so much scrutiny that she couldn't help but glance in his direction. She could tell that he wasn't buying anything that the man said. He suspected that they actually did know each other and Alexis knew that her face was giving him all the clues she needed. She had always been horrible at hiding things during face-to-face confrontations.

"Uh...Marc, can I speak to Alexis really quickly alone? I'm sorry; I don't mean to interrupt your dinner." Marc's eyes softened when he looked at Vanessa.

"Sure, go right ahead." He said. He flicked his eyes once more at Alexis and gave her another hard look. She knew that there would be a lot of explaining to do once she got to the house.

"Alexis...what is going on?" Vanessa asked once they were alone. Alexis gave her the wide-eyed "I don't know what you're talking about" look. She hoped that would fly with Vanessa, but she doubted it.

"I know you knew who that man was. What does he mean 'she still charges even if you don't do anything'? Is this what I think it is?" Vanessa asked narrowing her eyes on Alexis. Alexis bowed her head and looked down to the ground. She wanted to lie, but it was something about being questioned by her younger sister that was making her unable to do so. Vanessa sighed and looked back over towards her date.

"We need to talk, but it is going to take longer than the time that we have here. I will come over as soon as I can. Sometime this week." Vanessa said as she looked at her sister. Alexis was still averting her eyes. She was ashamed and she couldn't shake the feeling. She knew that Vanessa was smart enough to see through everything and come up with the truth.

"Fine." Alexis said quietly. Vanessa turned on her heels and headed back over to her date. Alexis began walking to her very visibly angry husband.

KAYLEN

"*W*hy the hell is she looking at me like that?" Kaylen asked Ra'Sheena as she sipped from her cup of coffee. After the morning that she had arguing with Caleb about rushing her off the phone right before she had to go to class and face exams, she was not in the mood for anyone's attitude.

"Who?" Ra'Sheena asked looking over the top of her thick glasses. Ra'Sheena was one of Kaylen's classmates and she was also one of the top students in their class. Kaylen had felt drawn to Ra'Sheena the first time she saw the awkward girl nearly two years ago when they took their first class together.

"That bitch...I mean, chick over there with the bad bleach blond weave. She needs to kill whoever did her hair like that." Kaylen said rolling her eyes in the direction of the target of conversation. Ra'Sheena turned to look and pushed her glasses up further on her nose. Kaylen stared at her for a minute and tried to resist shaking her head.

Ra'Sheena was about a good makeover away from being something that guys might actually stop and pay attention to. However, with the near unibrow, mixed with the uncombed hair she kept braided down in two French rolls and the clothes from the '90s, she was not winning in the men department.

Every day during breaks between classes and sometimes after class, Kaylen met with her to review material or just chat. Although Kaylen would rather gossip and chat more than go over material, Ra'Sheena normally seemed extremely out of her element when they discussed anything other than what they went over in class. Kaylen was unsure how Ra'Sheena planned on being a doctor when she still flinched every time someone said the word 'penis'.

"Oh, I know her. She is a year ahead of us, I think. Yeah, she's in her fourth year." Ra'Sheena pushed her glasses even further up her face and snorted. "Her name is Tameka, I think. She used to have a sister in our year but I think she got pregnant and dropped out."

"She was in medical school and didn't know how to use a condom?" Kaylen asked looking back at Ra'Sheena. Her friend's light brown face turned beat red and she looked down at the table.

"I...I...I don't know what happened. I just think she was pregnant and she left. Her boyfriend was in the program, though. I can't remember who he was." Ra'Sheena said still looking down at the table.

"Well, I don't know about all that shit, I'm just trying to figure out why her ass keeps staring at me like she has a problem!" Kaylen said looking back up and directly into Tameka's eyes. She widened her eyes and tilted her head at Tameka as if to say "What?" but Tameka only shot her another hard look before getting up to walk away.

"What do you think about the new professor?" Kaylen asked looking at Ra'Sheena who was turning red again.

"Well, he seems nice."

"He's kinda young, isn't he?" Kaylen sipped her coffee and continued looking at Ra'Sheena with a smile. She knew that Ra'Sheena had the hots for the new professor. She could tell by how she had nervously fumbled around to organize her notes when he walked in the class. The poor girl dropped everything, glasses and all, then sat there like Thelma from Scooby Doo feeling around for them until Kaylen made it over to help her.

"Yeah, he is young. I heard that he graduated high school early and started medical school during the time that most people would still be trying to finish their bachelors. He's very smart and he was the top of his class also. And..." Ra'Sheena's voice trailed off when she looked back at Kaylen. Kaylen had her head in her hands with her elbows rested on the table and she was thoroughly enjoying Ra'Sheena going on and on about a man...finally.

"Well, I haven't heard anything more about him than what you've heard, I'm sure." Ra'Sheena finished and then grabbed her cup to take a big, long gulp of her milk.

"Nah...you've heard a lot more than I know about him. I didn't know anything besides what he told us in class." Kaylen teased as she smiled at Ra'Sheena who was squirming nervously in her chair.

"Oh, yes. I like to know stuff about the professors so I googled him." Ra'Sheena said quietly. She ducked her head and Kaylen could see her smiling.

"You *like* him, Ra'Sheena! Just admit it!" Kaylen said playfully.

"He is nice. But that's all! Nothing more." Ra'Sheena placed her hand up for effect, but Kaylen didn't buy it.

"You know that's not true. Why don't you ask him for a little extra tutoring or something after class, if you know what I mean?" Kaylen smirked at Ra'Sheena and almost laughed out loud when she saw the look of horror that she got in return.

"No, I don't know what you mean and I *don't* need tutoring!" Ra'Sheena said putting her nose in the air.

"Well, damn, Ms. Smarty. I'm just trying to help." Kaylen was about to continue teasing Ra'Sheena but she saw someone approaching her out of the corner of her eye. She turned and there, standing right in front of her was Tameka.

"Can I help you?" Kaylen said with an attitude. She swung her legs up from under the table so that she wasn't pinned down underneath it if she had to move quickly.

"Is your name Kaylen?" The girl looked down at her with so much attitude that Kaylen felt the need to get up and speak with her eye to eye. She did not appreciate anyone looking down at her and she definitely did not appreciate the bad vibes that this girl was giving.

"Why?" Kaylen responded back folding her arms in front of her.

"Nevermind. That answers my question." The girl said looking her up and down.

"Bitch, is there a problem?" Kaylen said placing her hand on her hip and frowning up her face at Tameka.

"Not really. I was just wondering which bitch Caleb was dogging out now." Tameka said sneering down at her.

No, this bitch didn't! Kaylen reached back her hand to smack the shit out of her, but stopped short when Ra'Sheena grabbed her hand.

"Kaylen, no! This is not the place!" She whispered. Kaylen looked around and noticed that a few people, and other professors, had started observing the brief interchange.

"This ain't over, bitch!" Kaylen said as she grabbed her things and pushed pass a smug Tameka. She wanted to pound her face into the cement, but she figured that she risked too much doing that at the moment and she didn't want to get kicked out of school over no simple ass bitch.

"Tell Caleb to call me. We got shit to discuss." Tameka called behind her. Kaylen flipped her middle finger up in Tameka's direction as she walked away to class.

"I will let him call you if he needs someone to suck the leftover shit off his ass crack. Get the fuck out of here, hoe." Kaylen said as she walked away to class. Ra'Sheena followed behind looking red as a stop sign.

I can't believe this bitch tried me. But that will be the last time, I'm about to handle her ass now! Kaylen thought to herself as she followed Tameka's car away from Emory's School of Medicine. Kaylen had opted out of attending her last class just so that she could make sure that Tameka would be handled the way she needed to be. Disrespect was something that Kaylen wasn't having.

Kaylen watched Tameka's red Honda Accord turn into the entrance of an apartment complex near the campus and she turned right behind her. Student housing near Emory was expensive and

Kaylen wondered how Tameka was able to stay in a place as nice as the one she was pulling in to. She continued to follow Tameka's car around to the back of the complex where the single story apartments turned into two story townhomes with garages.

"Damn, this place is nice..." Kaylen said aloud as she looked around. Finally, Tameka pulled into one of parking spaces of a townhome that had a woman standing in front watching a little girl run around and play with a ball. Kaylen totally forgot about Tameka as her attention focused on the woman in the front of the house.

"Why the hell does she look familiar?" Kaylen said to herself as she continued to stare. She rolled down the window slowly so that she could get a better view and that's when it hit her. She knew who this chick was.

"That's that bitch Tiffany. Damn!" Kaylen said as her eyes darted to the right to focus on the little girl. Tiffany was someone who Caleb was messing with when Kaylen met him. Initially there had been a lot of tension between the two of them during the classes that they'd shared and at one point, Kaylen was ready to beat her ass. But then, one day Tiffany didn't show back up to class and Kaylen never thought about her again.

*She used to have a sister in our year but I think she got pregnant and dropped out...*Ra'Sheena's statement echoed throughout Kaylen's head as she looked back at the small girl playing in the yard. She couldn't be no older than about one or two years old. Kaylen squinted to take a better look at the little girl. She was dark brown, but other than that Kaylen wasn't close enough to see any resemblance to Caleb from where she currently sat. She was focusing so intently on the toddler that she did not notice that Tameka and Tiffany where looking directly at her.

"Shit...well, here we go." Kaylen thought when she noticed their gaze. She took off her seatbelt and started getting out of her car as Tameka started walking towards her.

"What the fuck are you doing here?" Tameka said walking up close to Kaylen and pointing in her face. Kaylen bit the inside of her lip as she tried to keep calm. Normally, she would have punched Tameka in the face for how she approached her, but Kaylen wanted to get to the bottom of some stuff first.

"To be honest, I followed your ass over here to speak about that shit that you pulled earlier. Why you so worried about Caleb anyways?" Kaylen said through clenched teeth. It was taking a lot of self-control to hold her arms down by her side instead of snatching the raggedy blond weave out of Tameka's head as she continued rolling her neck and eyes.

"Look," Tameka paused and the smug smirk that she had on her face made Kaylen's skin boil. She turned and glanced back towards Tiffany who was still staring over at them. She had picked up the young girl who was struggling to get down out of her arms to resume play. "I heard about you a while ago when you first started messing around with Caleb. I didn't know what you looked like or anything about you, but I did know that you are the bitch that Caleb started fucking while he was still with my sister."

Lord, help me to not slap the fire out of this b....

"That was over two years ago. Don't you think it's time for you to let that shit go? It's not any of your business anyways." Kaylen said rolling her eyes and placing her hand on her hip.

"Yes, it is my business. And the reason I'm stepping to you now is because everything was fine until Caleb told my sister the other day that he couldn't spend as much time over here with his *own damn baby* because he was in a so-called committed relationship with you. Oh... and also that he wouldn't be giving Tiffany money for her bills anymore since he had to take care of your grown ass." Kaylen struggled to keep her mouth from dropping to her toes as she realized that her suspicions were true. Caleb had a daughter. And this wasn't a secret daughter...apparently this was one that he knew about had been supporting even, and he didn't even bother to tell her.

"Yeah, that's right." Tameka continued as she watched her words sink in to Kaylen's brain. Anger started formulating in the pit of Kaylen's stomach and she began to get so angry that she could barely breathe.

Another motherfucker got me walking around here looking like a dumb ass bitch! Shit! Kaylen fought the urge to yell as she turned around and opened her car door.

"That's right. Go run and tell your no-good cheating ass nigga what I said. Be a good bitch and do that for me." Tameka laughed at Kaylen's back. Before she had time to get the last chuckle out of her throat, Kaylen turned around and back-handed her so hard that saliva splash out from between her lips. Tameka stumbled backwards and grabbed onto her face. Kaylen saw Tiffany run into the house to drop her daughter inside and two seconds later she was back out, running across the street towards them. Kaylen reached at her back and pulled out something that accompanied her whenever she left the house and it stopped them both in their tracks when they saw it.

"What you gonna do now, bitch?" Kaylen said looking over at Tiffany. She didn't point the gun at either one of them, but she did make sure that they saw it. She wasn't about shooting at someone when their baby was right in the house behind them, but she wasn't about getting her ass jumped either.

Kaylen took one last look at Tameka and Tiffany's shocked faces before turning to jump into her Lexus. She placed her gun on the passenger seat and then made a u-turn out of the neighborhood. Once she turned out of the complex, she let out a loud scream of frustration and sped down the street towards her house.

I am going to fuck Caleb's ass up.

JAZMYN

*J*azmyn was drumming her fingers across the oak arm of the Queen Anne chair in her living room when she heard the knocks on the door. She had been trying to figure out what to do about Trey Anderson. She had no problem with killing him, but she didn't think she could hide her cover if people around her just kept getting murdered. Either way, the situation had to be dealt with. The ring of the doorbell pulled her back into reality and she stood up from her chair.

Who could this be at the door? She had been spending so much time at Kingston's house that she figured that she shouldn't be getting any visitors here. Even her mail went to Kingston's address. No one knew that she still lived here. Jazmyn went to the desk near the front door and grabbed her knife before walking up to the door. Once she was close, she looked through the side window, instead of the peephole, to see if she could tell who it was at the door. Once she saw who it was, she sighed before dropping the knife back on the table and prepared to open the door.

"Vanessa? What are you doing here?" Jazmyn asked as she swung the door open. Vanessa was the last person that Jazmyn expected to see. Sure, she was Alexis' sister, but it wasn't like her and Jazmyn were close friends or anything. They talked in passing...but for the most part, they were too much alike to be friends. Both Jazmyn and Vanessa had a way with men that made them bend over backwards to give them everything they wanted, yet they both lacked the emotional connection to genuinely care for anyone. At least, Jazmyn had until she met Kingston. And as far as she knew, Vanessa had never experienced love; she was still happily romping lovelessly between the sheets with any eligible man who had the "equipment" to do the job properly.

"Hey, Jazmyn. I'm sorry for just showing up, but I didn't know how to explain to Alexis why I needed your number. I was hoping you would be home." Vanessa said. She looked extremely uncomfortable. Jazmyn stepped to the side to allow her to walk into the house.

"It's ok. Come right on in." Jazmyn flinched as she realized that what she'd said came out slightly more sarcastic than she had intended. She closed the door and walked behind Vanessa as she made her way to the living room. "Is there anything I can get for you? Water? Food?"

"No, actually, I really just want to get right to the point." Vanessa sat down on the sofa and stared down at her hands. She hesitated and took a deep breath before starting. "I know that you hang out with Dom. I need to speak with him." Jazmyn's head jerked around so fast to stare Vanessa in the face that she thought she may have got whiplash. She had been trained to expect the unexpected, as a lawyer and as a killer, but this was so far in left field that there was no way she could have anticipated it.

"What? What do you need to speak to Dom about?" Jazmyn asked Vanessa. What Dom did for a living was no secret. Most of Atlanta knew it, most of the east coast did, but no one could touch him so it didn't matter. But that reason alone was why Jazmyn was so shocked that Vanessa would be asking about Dom.

"He knows someone that I used to...someone I knew. I just want to talk to him about a few things. I need some closure." Jazmyn scrunched up her face into a frown as she looked at Vanessa.

This bitch is crazy. How could she possibly know anyone that Dom knows? He doesn't walk around in her upper class circles!

"Vanessa. Fucking around with Dom is something serious. You are asking me to contact him for you. You know who he is, so you should know why I need for you to dish me out some details and you need to start dishing them out pretty fast." Jazmyn said as she crossed her arms and sat back in her chair. Vanessa was asking for a big favor. Jazmyn was already in trouble with Dom and Crimson to begin with. She didn't need any more trouble from them. She watched as Vanessa stirred uncomfortably in her chair. Even in her current state of discomfort and anxiety, she was beautifully put together. Jazmyn took a second to admire her hair that fell in perfect curls down the side of her head. Her outfit was the right color to blend nicely against her cinnamon-brown colored skin. This is why they couldn't be friends. They would always be competing over the same dick.

"A while ago, I dated this guy named Ty. He was the head of a… group. A group called *The Family*." Jazmyn's eyes widened. She had heard about Ty. But she had no idea that Vanessa knew him….definitely not that she *dated* him. "Anyways, I was in love with Ty. He was the only person that I ever loved. He died some months after we got together. He killed the two leaders of a rival gang, 2-Fiyah, before he died." Vanessa sniffed and her eyes began to tear up.

Jazmyn hurriedly handed her the box of Kleenex that was sitting on the table and waited for her to continue her story. She couldn't believe what she was hearing. Everyone in The Disciples spoke about Ty and how he died. He went out like the ultimate Gangsta. He was the nigga that ate damn near a dozen bullets, but was still able to kill the two heads of the 2-Fiyah crew before he breathed his last breath. His legacy was one that most street niggas had heard about. And here Vanessa was talking about she was in love with him? Jazmyn was stunned into silence.

"After that happened, the two gangs joined together and formed one: The Disciples, which, I'm sure you know, is Dom's group. I knew Dom when he they called him Doom…before he took over The Disciples, that's what he went by. He was one of Ty's closest friends. I need

65

to talk to Dom because I'm thinking about trying to move on, but I feel guilty about it. I need to know what he thinks that Ty would say. I just need confirmation from another person that was close to him." Vanessa started crying and Jazmyn frowned up her face in disgust as she looked at her. She was never good at dealing with people's emotions, but she felt she should do something so she got up from her seat and walked over. She tried to give Vanessa a pretty awkward hug, but it didn't seem to help any, so she just backed up and sat back down in her seat.

"So, let me get this straight, Vanessa. You are telling me that Ty, the man that The Disciples speak about as if he was Jesus, the man that they recognize for unifying them...you're saying *you* used to date him?" Jazmyn rubbed on her forehead. This was not news that she thought she would be hearing today. Or any day for that matter.

"Yes. We dated when I was in high school. I was sixteen and he was eighteen. He was my first and only love. While he was dying, I swore to him that I would never love anyone ever again. I won't, but I'm thinking about dating. So I just need a second opinion from Dom." Jazmyn groaned inwardly. She had her own problems to deal with and did not want to get mixed up in this love bullshit.

"Hold on a minute, ok?" She asked. Vanessa nodded her head as she patted at her eyes with the tissue. Jazmyn grabbed her cellphone and walked to her bedroom. Once she was there, she closed the door and dialed Dom's number.

"Speak." Dom said once he answered the call.

"Do you know Vanessa? Alexis' younger sister?" Jazmyn asked.

"Yeah. Why?" Was all Dom said, but he said it in a way that made Jazmyn pause for a minute. His tone had completely changed from commanding to sympathetic.

Shit...maybe what Vanessa said was true. She dated Ty? What the fuck?

"She said that she dated someone named Ty. She needed to ask you something about him. She wanted your contact information so she could call you." There was a long pause after Jazmyn finished that statement.

"Give her my number." Was all he said, and then he disconnected the line. Jazmyn frowned and looked at the cellphone in her hand. She felt like she was in the twilight zone.

She walked back in to the living room and found Vanessa still patting at her eyes. She looked really tore up about something and Jazmyn almost felt sorry for her.

"Here, I will put Dom's number in your phone." Jazmyn said as she held out her hand for Vanessa's cellphone. Vanessa pulled it out of her purse and dropped it into her hand. Her eyes were puffy and rimmed with red and her nose looked slightly swollen. Jazmyn sighed heavily as she handed her back the cellphone after saving Dom's number. There was no way she could just kick her out of the house like this. It was time for a girl-chat.

"So...uh, how's Alexis doing?" Jazmyn asked. She felt the best way to stop Vanessa from crying would be to change the subject altogether. Plus, she hadn't heard from Alexis in a while and wanted to know what was going on with her.

"I don't know. I think she is getting mixed up in some crazy stuff. She's trying to deal with the rape on her own." Vanessa sniffed.

"So, she did admit that it was a rape?" Jazmyn sat back in her chair. Everyone had suspected that Alexis had been raped, but she had never confirmed it to anyone. Not that they knew of.

"Yes, she told me a while back." Vanessa said looking up at Jazmyn. Jazmyn squinted her eyes at Vanessa.

"She told you who did it?" Jazmyn asked Vanessa. Her heart started speeding up with anticipation. If Vanessa knew who had violated Alexis and she told Jazmyn, that would be the best news that she'd heard in a while.

And I'm in the right mood to go slice up a motherfucker, Jazmyn thought to herself.

"No..." Vanessa said quietly. Jazmyn sat up in her seat and tried to stop herself from grabbing Vanessa around her neck. She stared at her long and hard until Vanessa started to feel discomfort from her glare. She knew that Vanessa was lying. In her line of business, whether it was as a lawyer or a trained killer, it was important for her to be able to detect dishonesty. The lie was written all over Vanessa's face.

"You're lying. Who did it, Vanessa?" Jazmyn asked sternly. Vanessa flinched at Jazmyn's tone. Jazmyn would never hurt her, for the reason that she was Alexis' sister. But Jazmyn was a loyal friend to the end and she was ready to do whatever else was necessary to get the information out of Vanessa.

"She didn't want me to tell any..." Jazmyn jumped up and snatched Vanessa's cellphone out of her hand. She scrolled through the contacts until she got to where she had saved Dom's number.

"I did you a favor, Vanessa. You brought your ass over here asking me to contact Dom for you so you could rectify some situation that ain't have shit to do with me. Either tell me who the motherfucker is that did this or I'm deleting the shit out of your phone right now and you can take your puppy dog eyes and lovestruck woes back down the motherfucking street where you came from." Jazmyn looked down at Vanessa while holding the phone in her hand. She gave her a look that told Vanessa that she meant business. Vanessa looked up sadly and her eyes started to tear up again. Jazmyn sucked her teeth.

Damn it! I was supposed to stop this bitch from crying. Here she goes again!

"Who was it?" Jazmyn asked one last time.

"Dex....Dexter." Vanessa said quietly. Jazmyn wrinkled her eyebrows up at her. She couldn't have heard her correctly.

"Who?" Jazmyn asked again. Vanessa cleared her throat and looked up at Jazmyn.

"Dexter. Her friend from college." Jazmyn dropped the cellphone into Vanessa's lap and she turned around and walked over to her fireplace. She rested her hands on the mantle and tried to stifle her anger. She held so firmly onto the stone on the mantle that she thought that she might draw blood. She squeezed her eyes tightly as she tried to push away the memories of the night that Alexis was raped from her mind. What angered her so much was the fact that she was there when it happened. She had seen Dexter leaving out of a closet and he was adjusting his pants.

The motherfucker had just finished raping her! I could have ended his life right then! She was pissed because she had a feeling that something was not right, but she was so preoccupied with the drama going on with Kingston and Shanice that she had no idea that her friend had been hurt.

"I'm going to settle this shit. I put that on everything." Jazmyn whispered under her breath through her teeth. "I swear, if it's the last thing I do. I'm going to *handle* this motherfucker for this."

"What?" Jazmyn turned to look at Vanessa. She had almost forgot that the girl was sitting there. "Handle what? Are you ok?" Vanessa had concern in her eyes. Jazmyn nodded slowly and walked back over to where Vanessa sat.

"She ever said anything to you about where he is now?" Vanessa shook her head.

"No, but she told me when I called her the other day that he texted her…" This got Jazmyn's attention.

"He *texted* her? What did it say?" Jazmyn said as she sat down in her chair again.

"He said he was sorry. He said he was in Atlanta and wanted to apologize." Vanessa said, and then she looked quickly at Jazmyn. "Don't tell anyone though! Alexis and I have never been able to talk about anything, but for some reason she trusts me with this. If you call the cops or something and she gets dragged in to this, she will never forgive me!"

"Oh, I can promise you on everything that the police will not be involved. Your secret is safe with me." Jazmyn said before rising up from her seat. "I have to get some work done, Vanessa. I hope everything is ok with you now." Vanessa took the hint and started to gather her things before standing up.

"Yes. Thank you for your help."

"Anytime." Jazmyn said as she walked her to the door. Once Vanessa walked out, she locked the door and laid her back against it in deep thought. She had some work to do and she had to act quickly.

ALEXIS

"Ok. I'm ready. Tell me what's going on." Alexis just stared at Vanessa as she waited for her to start talking. Alexis really didn't know what to say to her. Vanessa was waiting for her to speak about the incident that had occurred last week with "John" at the restaurant. She didn't know how to start. How could she tell her sister that she was working at a whore house?

"There is nothing to tell." Alexi said and laid back on the bed, allowing her head to fall back on the stack of pillows behind her.

"I'm not going anywhere, Lex. So let's get this over with. I've got a few things to do later on today." Vanessa said looking at her watch. Alexis sighed. She did want to tell her sister. They had gotten closer over the last few months. Plus, there was something that she wanted to ask Vanessa about anyways.

"Remember when I got the abortion?" Vanessa nodded. "I met a friend there. She's a...she does things. But anyways, she introduced me to this lady, Ms. Juice." Alexis paused. She was losing her nerve. She needed to spit this out as fast as possible. "Ms. Juice owns a house that satisfies people's....er, um.....fantasies." Vanessa's eyes widened.

"Oh my God, Alexis! Tell me you are NOT having sex with men for money!" Vanessa yelled as she pulled back from her seat on the bed to take a closer look at her sister. Alexis "shushed" her, but it didn't matter. Marc had left the day after the restaurant incident. He decided that he wanted to return to work. Alexis didn't care…that meant she was able to come and go as she pleased without worrying about his questions.

"NO! I'm not having sex. There are some men that just want me to…hit them and, you know…slap them around and stuff. I do that." Vanessa's shocked face relaxed as she thought about Alexis' words and she smirked at her sister.

"Oh…you're into the S & M stuff, huh? I've had a few guys want me to do that to them." Vanessa laughed and Alexis joined in. "Hey, I don't blame you. That shit is therapeutic sometimes. Nigga do you wrong, sometimes you need to go beat someone else's ass." They continued laughing for a minute.

"I have something to ask you, Vanessa." Alexis started. Vanessa nodded her head and waited for Alexis to continue.

"You said at the restaurant that you were trying to date, but you didn't think you would ever fall in love again after Ty." Alexis paused and waited for Vanessa to respond. She didn't; she just nodded her head again. Alexis could see tears in her eyes and she immediately regretted asking about it.

Well, too late now, Alexis thought to herself. She decided to continue.

"Ty…he's the guy you dated in high school for a little while. What happened to him? I don't remember you mentioning him all that much." Vanessa paused for a minute. She seemed like she was deep in thought.

"I didn't mention him much because there was a lot going on that I couldn't talk about. He was….."

"SHHHHH! I heard someone downstairs." Alexis said putting her finger to her mouth. Vanessa's eyes widened and she stood up slowly and quietly. Alexis held up her finger and pointed when she heard a murmuring sound followed by deep, heavy laughter. "There it is again!" She whispered. Vanessa nodded her head. They both started creeping over to the entrance of the master bedroom. Once they got there, Alexis looked at Vanessa.

"You go first!" She said as she pointed out the door.

"Why do I have to go?" Vanessa pouted.

"Because I said so!" Alexis whispered back forcefully. Vanessa twisted up her face and put her hand on her hip.

"Get your ass out there, Vanessa!" She obeyed. Alexis followed close behind Vanessa as she started creeping down the hall and to the staircase. Suddenly, Alexis stopped cold in her tracks.

"Lex, c'mon, I can almost see who it is! Looks like Marc and a *fine* man! I can't really see though." Vanessa said peering over the open staircase and down to the first floor of the house with a big grin. But Alexis didn't need to go any farther. She had already heard him talking and she knew who it was. She felt all the blood drain from her face as she stood at the top of the stairs. The deep baritone voice that was coming from the downstairs sitting area was one that Alexis could never forget. She felt herself growing faint so she placed her hand on the banister of the stairs to steady herself.

"Lexi...?" Vanessa said as she ran back towards Alexis. "What's going on are you ok?"

"Hey, Lex, is that you? There is a surprise guest from the past here to see you!" Marc yelled up from the sitting area when he heard all the commotion.

"Marc! Come up here, now! Something is wrong!" Vanessa yelled as she tried to steady her sister. Alexis grabbed her stomach as she began to feel a sharp pang going through it. Thumps sounded through the house as Marc made his way up the stairs.

"Lexi! Are you ok?" Marc said running over to his wife. He grabbed her away from Vanessa and tried to pick her up.

"No! Don't touch me!" Alexis said snatching away from Marc.

"Lexi, what is going on?" Marc started to move back towards her and she panicked.

"Get away!" Alexis yelled as she backed away from him. She looked over to Vanessa who was standing with her mouth wide open from shock.

"Everything alright up there?" Dexter called from downstairs. Alexis turned towards his voice and she couldn't see anything but red as she stared at him over the top of the staircase. In place of the pain, embarrassment and guilt all she felt now was anger. She wanted to end his life in the same way that she felt he had nearly done to hers.

This man had violated her and then left like it was nothing. He was supposed to be one of her best friends, but instead he had become someone that she hated. Now months after the night he chose to desecrate her body, he was standing in her living staring at her as if nothing had happened. Asking her if everything was OK as if he wasn't the reason behind it all. Alexis couldn't stand there and take it anymore. She turned towards the stairs and rushed down as fast as her pregnant belly would allow.

"ALEXIS! What are you doing?" She heard Vanessa call from behind her as she followed down the stairs. Alexis glared at Dexter wanting nothing but to end his life. She had thought about this day a few times and wondered how it would go if it ever happened. How she would react if she ever came face to face with her rapist again. In her thoughts, her reaction had been cowardly and weak, but it wasn't like that today.

"Lex, I just wanted to say that I'm..." Dexter started as he moved towards her. Alexis' breathing sped up as she grew angrier and angrier. His movement caused the smell of his cologne to invade her nostrils and it took her back to the night that her baby was conceived out of pain and misery. Though she had gotten rid of it, she would never forget. She closed her eyes and tried to steady herself on the stairs as she felt pain in her chest.

"Lex, are you listening to me?" He touched her on her arm and that was it. Alexis grabbed a flower vase that sat on a mahogany desk at the base of the stairs and raised it above her head. Although the vase was very heavy and made of thick glass, Alexis held it with no problem. In one fluid motion, she brought it down directly against Dexter's skull. He crushed under the pressure and collapsed to the floor.

"Oh my God, baby...what are you doing? This is your friend...It's Dexter!" Marc said rushing to her side. "Vanessa, please help!" Alexis was standing still looking at Dexter who was lying on the floor with his eyes closed. He had a deep gash at the top of his head and blood was gushing from it.

"Lex?" Vanessa said pulling her attention. Alexis focused on her sister's worried expression. Out of the corner of her eye, she could see Marc tending to Dexter. "It's ok. We can deal with this the right way. Not like this, Lex. Not like this!" Alexis continued to stare at Vanessa who had tears in her eyes. "We can call the police. You will be safe."

Alexis' eyes darted over to Marc who was bent down assisting Dexter whose eyes were starting to flutter. He was not dead. This was too much for her to take. This realization made her feel like her air supply had been cut off. She had to get out of there.

Alexis ran to the bar area near the living room and grabbed the car keys she saw on the table, then bolted out of the door as fast as she could.

"Alexis, wait!" Vanessa called behind her, but Alexis slammed the door shut in her face and ran towards her white Range Rover. She pressed the button to automatically unlock it, opened the door, and jumped inside. She was about to pull out of the driveway when she noticed that Dexter's electric blue Camaro was parked in front of her. She squeezed her eyes shut as she thought about what happened the last time she rode with him in that vehicle. Vanessa had made it out of the house and was tapping lightly on the driver side window, but Alexis could barely hear it. She grabbed the steering wheel tightly and gritted her teeth together as she tried to wipe away the mental images that were invading her brain.

Flashbacks of Dexter slamming away on top of her began to take over. She could remember the sounds he made, the way he had ripped her clothes out of the way and even the way he had grabbed her around the throat, forcing her not to move.

Alexis looked up at his car, and then threw her own vehicle into 'reverse'. She mashed on the gas as hard as she could and the Range sped backwards, causing Vanessa to be flung backwards into the grass. Alexis could see out her peripheral that Marc had finally made it out of the house and was trying to figure out what was going on as he ran towards her. She slammed the SUV into 'drive' and mashed on the gas again as hard as she could. The vehicle burst forward and accelerated quickly. Alexis closed her eyes and braced for the impact as she pummeled into the side of the Camaro. The crack of the two metals colliding was the last thing that invaded her mind as she fell into unconsciousness from the impact of her head hitting the top of the steering wheel.

&

ALEXIS' EYES FROWNED AS SHE HEARD THE BEEPING.

What the hell is that noise? Damn...my head is killing me! She heard murmuring of someone talking so she decided to lie still. She slowly opened one eye only enough to try to see what was around her. The white walls with the cheap wallpaper, small wall-mounted TV and the horribly uncomfortable flat bed clued her in on the fact that she must have been in the hospital. She could smell the scent of disinfectant mixed with the scent of sick people in the air and it made her stomach turn. She hated the hospital.

"Well, where is that guy now?" Duchess asked.

"Dexter? I don't know. He left as soon as he came to. I asked him if he wanted to go to the hospital or something".

"You don't think he's the guy who did *it* to her, do you?" Duchess whispered.

"No, he is one of her best friends. He introduced us. Plus, he is gay. He wouldn't do anything to hurt her." Marc sighed. "Plus, you know she never actually said that anything happened to her that night." Alexis heard Duchess scoff at Marc's last comment. Alexis felt the shame, guilt and humiliation returning as she listed to them speak.

"Well, why would Alexis attack him? That's not like my daughter. She is not a violent person." Horace said. Silence followed as everyone thought about the question.

"Alexis has been acting funny with me, also. Sometimes she looks at me like I'm not her husband. I think something about what happened has made her distrustful of men in general. I think she attacked him based on that reason alone." Marc said quietly. Alexis could hear the pain in his voice and she knew that he was struggling to keep it together.

"When are they going to be able to tell us how she is doing?" Kaylen was here? Alexis was mortified. Now she would have to endure her friends treating her as if she were a crazy lady as well.

"The doctor should be back soon." Jazmyn was here, too. Did Marc call everybody?

Alexis cleared her throat and opened her eyes. All attention went to her as they tried to gauge how long she may have been awake.

"Lexi, how are you feeling? The doctor said that you would probably be asleep for a while. I'm surprised you are awake." Marc said rubbing the top of her head.

"Stop, Marc. It hurts…" Alexis said closing her eyes tightly.

"Alexis, I know that you've had a rough day. But, honey, we need you to talk about some things." Duchess said walking over to her side. She looked at Marc sharply and he followed her unspoken demand for him to move out of the way.

"Why did you attack Dexter? Is he the one that did "you know what" to you?" Duchess let her eyes roll over her body as she asked the last question. She made it seem like Alexis had a disease. Alexis looked over to Horace who was staring at his daughter with so much love, care and sympathy that she felt like she would cry. Alexis looked around the room at everyone's expressions. Kaylen, Vanessa, Jazmyn Marc and even Duchess, all of them, had sympathetic looks in their eyes. They all felt bad for her and she hated the feeling of being pitied.

"No. It wasn't him." Alexis said quietly. Everyone let out the breath they had been holding. Everyone except Jazmyn. She was looking at Alexis with a stare that said one word: bullshit.

"I need to speak to Lexi alone, please. Legal stuff." Jazmyn said. Marc looked at Alexis with an unspoken question in his eyes.

"It's ok, Marc. You can go ahead." Marc looked back at her intensely.

"Lex, after you are done speaking with Jazmyn, I will be back. We need to talk." Alexis nodded her head as she watched everyone walk out of the room. Jazmyn kept her eyes on Alexis' face and the hard stare made her squirm with discomfort.

"You're lying." Was all she said. Alexis did not respond. She rolled over on her side and put her back to Jazmyn. "So it's Dexter. I remember seeing him the night of Zo's party...walking out of a room, adjusting his pants." Alexis turned to face her.

"Yes. It was him." Alexis whispered.

"Alexis, listen to me. I can promise you right now that you will never have to worry about this motherfucker ever again if you don't want to." Jazmyn came closer and looked her directly in the face stared back at her. She seemed deep in thought as Alexis looked at her.

"How? He showed up at my home today and I wasn't even expecting that. How can you promise that?" Alexis asked.

"Don't worry about it. Do you care what happens to him?" Jazmyn said as she turned to sit down on the bed next to Alexis.

"Fuck, no. I hope he rots in hell." Alexis responded louder than she had originally intended.

"Consider it done." Jazmyn rose up off the bed and walked out of the room.

Consider it done? What does she mean? Alexis thought. She heard the door open again and the next person she saw was Marc.

He walked in looking incredibly stressed, like the weight of the universe was on his shoulders, and Alexis couldn't blame him. She knew that her parents were probably giving him hell for everything that was happening to her. In reality, none of it was his fault. She knew that he wanted to help her, but he didn't know how. This was the first time that they had endured any kind of issue in their marriage because Alexis had always been accommodating to whatever he had wanted. Now he was in a situation that he didn't know how to deal with and the stress of it all showed on his face.

"Lexi, we need to talk now." Marc said as he sat down in the chair next to the bed. He pulled it forward and rested the palms of his hands on the bed near her.

"What do you want to talk about?" Alexis turned on her back and stared up at the television screen. She was afraid that her eyes would covey her feelings and she didn't know if she was ready for that.

"I know you were raped. You've never admitted that shit to me, but I know it. I'm not crazy. Not saying it doesn't make it true." Alexis cut her eyes at Marc. She had never heard him curse. She wasn't sure if it was the fact that he was tired or that he was probably annoyed with her parents, but he was also speaking with a roughness that she had never heard before. His voice was deeper and raspier. He had her full attention.

"I've given you time. I haven't really pressed you about the rape since it happened. I've been waiting for you to open up and speak to me, but you haven't. I asked you who did this to you and you avoid it." Marc clenched his jaw before he continued speaking. "Now, I want you to tell me. Who *the fuck* did this to you?" Alexis mouth dropped slightly as she looked at Marc.

Damn. I didn't know he had it in him!

"Ma..ma...Marc. I...uh...." Alexis stuttered as she tried to think of a way to get herself out of this situation.

"Enough of the bullshit, Alexis. I'm done playing the part of the piece of shit husband. You have been...someone did something to you and you are going to tell me about it now." Marc spoke to forcefully that Alexis held her eyes wide open as she looked at this new man in front of her. She could see the anger in his face and it almost looked like he was about to lose control. There was a vein throbbing on his temple, almost eclipsed by his dark brown hair. Marc looked like he was The Hulk in the midst of a transformation.

This is Marc motherfuckin' 2.0! Shit got me hot.

"Dexter." Alexis said so quietly that she was certain that Marc couldn't even hear her. But she knew he had when she saw his face slowly transform from pure rage and frustration to a mix of shock, guilt, and confusion.

"Dexter? Dexter did this?" Marc repeated. His eyes were no longer looking at her, but pass her, as if he were in deep thought. Alexis nodded her head slowly as she saw tears rise up in the corners of his eyes. She watched as Marc began clenched his jaw tightly again. She knew in his silence that he was thinking over the day's events. How he had let Dexter into his home. How he hadn't killed him when he had the chance. Suddenly, Marc rose up quickly from his chair and started moving towards the door.

"Marc, wait!" Alexis called out behind him.

"Lexi, I love you." That was the last thing he said to her before he walked out of the door.

KAYLEN

Kaylen threw her phone into the passenger seat and groaned loudly. She had been trying to call Caleb ever since she had left the hospital. Now that she was sure that Alexis was fine, the next thing on her list was having a big discussion with Caleb on whether or not what Tameka had told her was true.

"How the fuck can he expect to be able to hide a baby from me? We live in the same damn city! Shit! Isn't this something he should have told me before he decided to give me this damn ring?" Kaylen stopped at the red light and looked down at the 5-carat princess cut diamond ring that Caleb had given her. The diamond was flawless, but she felt stupid for wearing it. She slid it off her finger and threw into the middle console area in her car.

Kaylen was about to crank up her radio loud to let off steam when she heard her cell phone chime. She reached over and grabbed it off the seat before pulling away from the intersection. She glanced down and saw the text was from Zo.

Shit! I forgot all about him coming over tonight! Kaylen looked at the clock on the dash and saw that it was only about four o'clock. She still had a little time to get things together before he came over. She pressed the button on the phone and peeked at the text as she turned into her subdivision.

Still on for tonight? Though it wasn't anything big, the message still brought a smile to Kaylen's face. She placed the phone down on her lap and turned into the driveway. She responded as she waited for the garage door to rise.

Yes...what time? 7-ish? Kaylen figured five hours would be enough time to get everything together before Zo came over. She still felt a little bad that she would be entertaining him while she was engaged to Caleb, but it wasn't that bad of a feeling that she was going to swap up her plans.

Kaylen drove the car into the garage and pressed the button for it to close behind her. She turned it off and was about to get out when she heard her phone chime again.

I will be there. Can't wait to see you. Kaylen smiled at the text as she unlocked the door and walked into the house. The first thing she noticed was that the alarm did not chime and she wondered if she had forgotten to turn it on that morning before she left. It was possible.

"Tiny?" Kaylen looked around for her dog but she heard nothing. She started walking up the stairs to see if Tiny was upstairs. As she approached the bed rooms, she heard scratching coming from one of the guest rooms. Kaylen closed her eyes and took a deep breath. She felt the hairs on the back of her neck rise up as she exhaled slowly. She reached down to grab the knob and opened the door slowly.

As soon as she opened it, Tiny burst out of the room and ran past her. Kaylen relaxed and tried to steady her breathing.

"Tiny! How did you close yourself up in this room? What were you doing in here any..." Kaylen's voice trailed off as her eyes caught something sitting on the dresser in the guest room. "How did this get here?" Kaylen said to herself as she walked over to the dresser. She looked down and grabbed the tiny silver objects that had caught her eye.

Cufflinks. They were black cufflinks that she had bought Salem as a present once they had been officially dating a month. Kaylen felt a chill rising up her back as she looked at them. There was no explanation for how they had gotten there. She hadn't left anything of Salem's in her home when she returned from jail. Everything that belonged to him had been thrown out.

Maybe somehow these made it through. Maybe Caleb saw them and put them here. Kaylen wasn't ready to think of any other possibilities.

"Speaking of Caleb...." Kaylen pulled out her phone once again and dialed Caleb's number. She was just about to hang up the phone when she heard some shuffling on the other end as he answered the phone.

"Kay? What's going on? I'm in the middle of a..."

"I spoke to Tameka and Tiffany today." Kaylen said slowly. There was a long pause as she waited for Caleb to speak.

"Hold on a minute. Let me walk out of this seminar." Kaylen rolled her eyes to the ceiling and placed her hand on her hip as she waited for him to return to the call.

"Hey. So...um, what do you mean you spoke with Tam..." Caleb started slowly.

"Don't act stupid, Caleb. When were you going to tell me that you have a daughter?" Kaylen yelled into the phone. She paused as she waited to see how Caleb would respond. At this point, the only thing he could do was to deny or own up to it.

"Kaylen, listen. I was going to tell you. I just was looking for..."

"The right time?" Kaylen finished for him with sarcasm. "Don't you think this is something that should have been said before the proposal? Or any other time within the last eight months?"

"Well...I...uh...listen, Kay." Caleb sighed loudly. Kaylen listened on the other end, ready to hear the excuse that he was thinking up.

And it better be good, she thought to herself.

"Yes, Caleb?"

"I really just wanted to wait for the right time to talk to you about all this, Kay." Caleb sighed again.

"Well, you still fucking around with her, too, Caleb?" Kaylen was infuriated. She felt stupid, once again, and Caleb didn't even seem to have a decent excuse for his actions.

"What? Kaylen...no! I'm not doing..."

"What about Shaun? Had a nice dinner? Oh and I'm sure you've caught up with Nikki, too, right?" Kaylen yelled into the phone.

"Uh...Kay, you need to calm down. There is nothing going on." The more Caleb denied the more pissed off Kaylen became at him. She clenched her teeth together and pulled the phone away from her ear. After pressing the "end call" button, she slipped the phone into her pants' pocket. She was so upset that she had totally forgotten to ask him about the cufflinks.

KAYLEN WAS JUST FINISHING UP THE LAST FEW BITS OF CLEANING WHEN she heard the doorbell ring. She felt her heart thump in her chest and her palms immediately became sweaty. The anxiety rose up and she felt her throat start to clench up.

Damn, why does he have this effect on me? She thought as she stopped at the mirror near the front door to check out her hair. Her hair was still cut in a short bob style and it looked fine, but it wasn't perfect. She pulled at the ends and tried to smooth down her edges. Kaylen groaned inwardly at the result. She tried using her nails to rake at her hair, but her edges didn't budge.

"Why didn't I just go see Nesha today?" She whispered to herself.

Oh, well... Kaylen unlocked the door and grabbed the doorknob. She pulled the door open and almost passed out. There, directly in front of her, stood Zo, looking better than she had ever seen him. She could tell that he hadn't missed a day at the gym over the past five months. He was more muscular than he had been before. He had lost a little weight, but he'd made up for it with muscle mass. He was wearing a thick white t-shirt with sleeves that hugged perfectly around his muscular arms. His jeans were crisp, clean and new. They hung at his waist in a way that made Kaylen wonder about what was underneath. He had a fresh cut and his skin looked like smooth toffee. He was effortlessly sexy. There was no other way to describe it. And Kaylen hadn't even bothered to get her hair done. She tried to muster up a smile as she pressed her hands down her slightly wrinkled tank top and sweat pants.

Damn!

"Hi Zo! C'mon in." Kaylen said as she moved to the side to allow him to walk into her home. "Here I will show you over to the kitchen." Zo paused as he waited for her to close the door.

"This is a pretty nice place." He looked at her gently and then raised one eyebrow. "I don't have to worry about no shit going down from my being in here, right?" Kaylen walked over to him and grabbed the bag of food from his hands.

"No, Caleb is out of town. And you and I are just friends, anyways...right?" Kaylen paused during her walk to the kitchen to turn back and look at Zo as she waited for an answer. A slow nod was his only response. Kaylen continued walking into the kitchen and placed the food on the countertop. She reached into the cabinet and pulled out two plates and two glasses.

"So how have you been?" Zo asked as he pulled out a barstool and sat down at the bar. "It's been a while since we caught up." He grinned a little while he spoke and his deep dimples made butterflies flutter in Kaylen's stomach. She glanced over at him and caught him just as he let his eyes drop to take a look over her body. Without thinking, she held her breath and sucked in her stomach a little.

Damn! Why does he make me so nervous?! Kaylen said as she turned away from him to walk over to the refrigerator. She opened it up and grabbed two Cokes out for them to drink.

"You ok with soda?" Kaylen asked walking over to Zo.

"Yeah, that's good." He said, holding out his hand for the drink. He stared at her so intently as if he were waiting for something. Kaylen's breath caught up in her chest as she returned his gaze.

Oh, shit...he is waiting for me to answer his question!

"Oh, well...I'm good. I mean, Caleb and I have been doing ok... together. He proposed a while ago. You know that, right?" Kaylen passed him the soda and then raked her hands once again through her hair. She was nervous and almost on the verge of babbling and she knew it. She looked over at Zo and he was staring at her with a smirk teasing the edges of his lips. She felt embarrassed by the fact that he seemed so amused.

"Yes, I think I heard at some point about your...engagement." Zo's eyes continued to shine with laughter as he popped the top off the Coca Cola can and began drinking it. Kaylen started putting food on the plates as he drank. She did not want to discuss Caleb with Zo and she was annoyed with herself for bringing him up in the first place. "You love him?" Something about the way Zo asked her made her get so hot. She looked up at him and noticed that the smirk was gone and he had the most serious expression on his face that she had ever seen.

"I...uh, I care about him a lot. It's just...we have issues." Kaylen looked back down at the food as she spoke. She glanced back up Zo as she continued shoveling food onto the plates and noticed that the smirk had returned along with the glitter in his eye.

"You care about him. That's it. But you're going to marry him?" Zo rose up from the barstool and walked over to her. Kaylen placed the carton of food down, along with the utensils she had been using, and turned to face him.

"Yes. I think, anyways. That's what we planned." Kaylen sucked in a breath suddenly when Zo moved closer to her and she could smell his cologne. It had a deep, dark, manly smell to it. It was strong and very masculine. Kaylen loved it and she tried to steady herself on her feet as she felt her pussy react to the scent by thumping against her panties.

"So, you're just going along with the plan?" Zo was so close that Kaylen could almost taste the mint chewing gum that he had in his mouth. As he spoke, she felt the cool air blow against her and she nearly buckled with excitement. She wanted to answer Zo's question, but she couldn't because he had gotten so close to her face that the only thing she needed to do was pucker her lips and kiss him right on the mouth. So that's exactly what she did.

When Kaylen pressed her lips against Zo's, the first thing that she felt was a rush of emotion. Longing, wanting, needing...all the things that she had felt for him before everything went down with Salem. He had always been the one that she preferred. If Salem hadn't approached her first that night, she knew her life would have went differently.

Kaylen felt flutters in her chest when Zo pushed his tongue between her lips. She opened her mouth and eagerly accepted it inside. He explored her mouth with such patience, care and desire that she felt herself growing a little weak. She felt him wrap his arms around her to steady her and she fell into his embrace. Zo cupped her from underneath, picked her up quickly and carried her over to the barstool. He made sure to not break their kiss as he sat her down gently and pulled her in close to him. She was pressed so closely to him that she could swear she felt the light thumping of his heart beating against her chest. His cologne aroused her. It had a manly scent, but there was a roughness about the smell that excited her. She wanted more of him…all of him. There was nothing that she wanted more than for him to pull off all her clothes and seduce her. There was no way the sex wouldn't be good…their chemistry was perfect. The vibe they had was strong and it felt right. She knew that having him inside of her would be the icing on the cake.

Kaylen moaned when she felt Zo glide his hand over her chest. The faint touch made her nipple rise and grow tender against his touch. She was in heaven…for all of about two more seconds before her phone rang.

Kaylen groaned when she realized from the ringtone that it was Caleb. Zo pulled away from her and stuck his hands in his pockets as he backed away. Kaylen looked at him for a moment before grabbing her phone. She was about to press the button to answer the call, but decided against it. She was not in the mood to hear anymore of his excuses. She pressed the "ignore" button and threw her phone on the counter. She looked back at Zo who was staring at her silently.

"So….are you ready to eat?" Kaylen asked him, looking over to the food that was on the counter.

"Yeah, I could eat." Zo responded, still standing with his hands in his pants pocket.

"Ok, well let me just warm up the food real quick." Kaylen said walking over to the plates.

"It's ok. I'm cool with it as is," Zo said as he walked over towards her. He grabbed one of the plates and bit off a piece of the eggroll as he walked over to the dining room table. "It's perfect."

Kaylen watched as he sat down, said a quick silent prayer and continued eating. She shook her head from side to side as she laughed to herself.

You can take the man out the hood, but not the hood out the man, Kaylen thought as she grabbed her plate and went to sit across from Zo at the table.

"So Caleb..." Zo said between bites. He looked at her with his eyebrows raised, so Kaylen figured it was the beginning of a question although it sound like a statement.

"Yes?" Kaylen said, shoving a spoonful of chicken fried rice into her mouth.

"Can I ask you a question?" Zo said placing his spoon down on his plate. He seemed a little frustrated and it caught Kaylen's undivided attention. She paused mid-chew and dropped her spoon onto her plate. She nodded her head slowly and waited for Zo to speak.

"Why are you still with that nigga?" Zo bought his arms forward and leaned forward on the table as he waited for her to answer his question.

"Well...we are getting married. So..." Kaylen's voice trailed off as she tried to find a suitable response.

"Do you not remember what just happened a few minutes ago? You just kissed me." Zo said as he pointed at himself, square in the chest. "You sure you ready to be his wife?" Kaylen paused as she thought about what he'd just said.

"So you're saying that I shouldn't marry him?"

"I'm saying that you know you shouldn't marry him. He's not the one. He's your fallback after Salem." As soon as Zo said his name, it seemed like the air was sucked out of the room. Kaylen watched as Zo's face went totally blank.

"Are you ok?" Kaylen asked him. "Have you been ok since that night?" She really wanted to know. She knew that part of the reason that she had not heard from Zo had to be what went down with Salem.

"I'm good." Was all he said. Zo cleared his throat before picking up his spoon again and starting back eating. "So, what happened with the jail thing? You still have to go to court or something?"

"No, it's over. They released me and dropped the charges." Zo stopped chewing and looked up at me with confusion.

"They just dropped the charges? That's it...no explanation as to why?" Kaylen shrugged. She hadn't even thought about getting an explanation as to why the charges were dropped. She was just happy they were dropped.

"No. I didn't ask about it either. I was happy to be out of jail." Zo stared at her for a while as he thought about what she'd said.

"They don't just drop charges, Kay. There has to be a reason." He said after his long pause. Then he shrugged and picked up his fork. "Anyways, I don't want to think about all that. I'm worried about you and how you've been carrying on since then. How have you been?" Kaylen looked at him and sighed. Something about him made her trust him like she would a best friend. She sat down and exhaled heavily.

"Not good. There's a lot going on with me and Caleb. I'm trying to figure out how I got into this shit so deep." Kaylen stopped and looked up at Zo. He wasn't eating. He was staring at her deep in her eyes. She felt her heart flutter a little in her chest. The scent of his cologne seeped again into her nostrils from where he sat across the table. It was a powerful elixir and she wanted nothing more than to be closer to him.

Zo stood up and walked over to her chair. He grabbed her hand and pulled her up so that she was standing right in front of him. She looked up at him and glanced away quickly. There was no way that she would ever be able to get used to the way that Zo made her feel when he looked at her. His stare was so intense and so deep that she felt love coming from him.

Is that even possible? He doesn't know enough about me to love me, Kaylen thought. But it didn't matter. Love is what she felt when he looked at her. He spoke to her through his eyes; he didn't even have to say a word for her to know how he felt.

"Kay...I missed you." Zo said quietly. He said it so low that Kaylen thought for a minute that he hadn't meant for her to hear him. Kaylen looked up at him again and saw that he was still staring at her so intensely. She knew at that moment that something was about to happen. And it did.

The kiss came before Kaylen even had proper time to react. It caught her completely off guard...but in a good way. Zo's lips pressed onto hers with such care and gentleness that she felt weak in the knees. He reached around her and grabbed her around her waist, pulling her closer to him. Kaylen responded by wrapping her arms around his neck and deepening their kiss. This was the moment that she had been waiting for. Although she had kissed him before, this time it was different. The timing was better. Sure, she was still with Caleb, but he had so many secrets that she wasn't sure she really knew where that relationship was heading. Or if they even had a relationship at all.

Kaylen jumped slightly when she felt Zo cup her ass and pull her in even closer to him so that she was pushed up on top of the bulge in his pants. She sucked in a breath and inhaled the scent of his skin deeply. Zo didn't miss a beat; he ducked his head down and started sucking on her neck gently. Kaylen placed her hand on the back his head and pushed in closer into her. It was as if they had been wanting each other from a distance for so long that now that the moment had arrived, she didn't just want him kissing the surface of her skin; she wanted him to be a part of her. No matter how much she pulled him in, she wanted him deeper. He seemed to feel the same way because the grip that he had on her was just short of painful as he hugged her towards him and sucked hard on her neck. Kaylen felt her skin burning where he was sucking and she knew that passion marks were inevitable.

"I want to taste you." Zo whispered in her ear. Kaylen felt her muscles that made up her soft folds begin to contract in response to his request. Her sweet secretions oozed out of her and made her panties cling to her skin. She exhaled slowly as she contemplated his request. This moment had been a long time coming. There had been days when, although she was lying right next to Caleb, all she could think about was how much she wanted him to be Zo. The attraction levels between them were so high that sometimes she felt as if her oxygen was affected by it. She always seemed a little short of breath in his presence, as if him being around sucked away the breath from her lungs. It was a crazy connection that they had and she really couldn't describe it. At this moment she didn't want to describe it either. She just wanted to *feel* it.

"Please." Is all that she could muster out. Though one word, it seemed to satisfy Zo. He leaned over and kissed her deeply as he pulled down her sweatpants. Kaylen returned his kiss and thanked God that she had made sure to put on her favorite lingerie set. She may have been in sweatpants, but she felt confident in knowing that as soon as he took off the clothes, she would look perfect.

As soon as he slipped her pants over her feet and let them dropped to the floor, he slipped one finger inside of her panties. He raised one eyebrow and looked up at Kaylen intently. She simply stared back at him as she held her breath. It wasn't as if she wanted to do it, it was just a natural response to what she was feeling. His finger rubbed softly against her and it sent an electric shock of pleasure through her to the point that she shuddered against him. He smirked when he felt it and Kaylen felt herself dripping more of her juice as she looked at him. He pushed two fingers deep inside of her and with the other hand started pulling her panties down smoothly. Kaylen leaned back and let her head fall backwards as she enjoyed the sensation of him running his fingers back and forth inside of her. She opened her thighs a little farther as I sign that he was welcome to place more fingers in. She wanted more of him and at that moment, he could have asked for anything and he would have gotten it.

Suddenly she felt him pull out his fingers from inside her and she tried to fight the disappointment that started rising up in her. This was the way it seemed to always be with him. He would start something, then all of a sudden, his conscious would come out of nowhere and he would stop.

*Fuck! I'm tired of that shi…..*Kaylen's thoughts were cut short when she felt Zo's tongue flick across her clit.

"Oh, daaaammmnnn….." she moaned. This was not what she was expecting. She just knew that he was ready to quit on her. But here he was….his tongue was now pushing deep inside her with a hunger that she had not known he'd had for her. She spread her legs open as wide as she could and pressed up against him when he started to suck hard on her most sensitive area. She had her eyes closed so tightly that she could see stars through the darkness of the back of her eyelids. The tingling sensation that was rising up in her was so strong that she squeezed her toes tightly in response to the feeling. Zo pulled back off of her clit and she let out a heavy breath as she tried to regain control of her breathing. But Zo wasn't concerned about allowing her time to recuperate. She shivered and twitched when she felt him start to blow cold air onto the area that he had just sucked almost to a climax. Kaylen moaned loudly and she felt herself nearing an orgasm.

Shit. This nigga is about to make me cum and he isn't even touching me! Kaylen pulled her head up and looked down at him. There was nothing better than watching the most sexiest man that she had ever seen kneeling with his head between her legs, with both of his hands cupping her ass and pulling her pussy into his face. She felt weak and she couldn't stand to watch him any longer. The sight was too much for her and she wasn't sure about how long she could hold out. The excitement was taking over; that mixed with the electricity pulsing through her body from his touch, was almost too much for her to handle at the moment. Zo pushed forward and sucked her clit back into his mouth with such ease that it almost seemed that she was magnetically attracted to him. This feeling was everything.

Zo started kissing her pink folds as if he were tongue kissing her. He flipped his tongue over and through her with so much care that Kaylen knew that there was no way in hell that he hadn't been thinking and dreaming about this moment as much as she had. He pressed against her ass and pulled her in closer to him, taking more of her into his mouth. She moaned at the feeling...the gushing sounds that were coming from her started bringing out the freak in her and she started to grind her hips against his face. He moaned in pleasure as she started pressing up closer to him and he responded by licking, kissing and sucking more feverously. Kaylen was about to cum. She wanted nothing more at that moment than for him to keep going forever. She started grinding against him even more so and he continued rolling and flipping his tongue in her. He sucked and licked and sucked and blew on her throbbing clit. Then he stopped.

Kaylen jerked her head to look at him.

What's going on? Kaylen thought to herself. *I know he is not trying to stop!* Kaylen looked at him with a confused stare, but he still continued to look at her with a blank stare.

"What's wrong?" She asked him. Whatever it was, she knew that it better be a damn good reason for him to feel as if he needed to interrupt her when she was on the verge of ecstasy.

"Are you sure about this?" Zo asked her, looking deep into her with his brown eyes.

"Yes. I am." Zo sat and looked at her for a minute as if he were trying to analyze if she was certain. After what felt like forever, although it was probably a few seconds, Zo looked down and sighed. Kaylen clenched her jaw. She was pissed. But it didn't last long, because the next second, Zo swooped her up in his arms and started carrying her towards the living room. She wrapped her legs around his body and placed her arms around him. She let her face bury deep in his neck and she inhaled the scent of his cologne. He was the perfect man. Everything about him was exactly what he needed.

Zo walked over to the sofa in the living room and pulled off the afghan that she kept on it for when she needed something to throw over herself when she sat down in here. Caleb was always warm and she was always cold, so she kept it in here for that reason. Happily, it seemed that her afghan was going to be used for a different reason this time. Zo continued to hold her as he used one hand to flip the afghan onto the plush olive colored carpet in the living room. After he was satisfied with how it was spread out, he knelt down and laid

Kaylen gently onto the top of the sheet. Kaylen waited with excitement for what would come next. She'd had sex plenty of times in the past, but it was something about this experience that made her so nervous that she almost felt like a sixteen year old girl with no sexual experiences at all.

Zo stood up and walked over to the light switch and flicked it off. Kaylen loved candles and always made sure to have some lit because she loved to have the smell of lavender permeating around the room. When Zo turned off the lights, the soft flicker of the candles gave the room a romantic feel and it only excited Kaylen even more. She was ready for this moment. She had envisioned it in her mind's eye for so long and it was finally here.

Zo pulled off his shirt first and Kaylen took her time admiring his body. He had definitely been working out in the gym. His washboard abs were something to be envied by every man and appreciated by every woman. Kaylen imagined herself running her tongue up and down them as he pushed into her. It was a beautiful sight.

Next he slipped off his pants and boxers in one motion and Kaylen sucked in a big breath. He was standing fully at attention and Kaylen was extremely impressed.

Nothing like a beautiful dick that makes a bitch wanna jump on it with the quickness. Zo looked at her without saying a word and Kaylen knew that he was giving her one last chance to back out. Kaylen responded to him by sitting up on her elbows and letting her legs fall all the way open, giving him the perfect view of her sweet cherry. She smiled when she saw his eyes drop down and run over the visual she was offering up. He licked his lips and then knelt down to drink more of her. Kaylen fell back flat onto the floor as the feeling of pleasure totally consumed her. Zo was between her legs taking gulps as if his life depended on it. She was convinced that he considered her a fountain and intended to drink everything that she was offering up to him. And she had a lot to offer. The sweet juice did not stop running from out of her; the more he sucked, the more she gave.

Kaylen wanted to moan, but she couldn't catch her breath. She wanted to grind up against him, but she was frozen into place. He was gripping her so tightly that she could not move. The only thing she could do was enjoy the sensation of his tongue running up and down her clit as if he were playing the keys on a xylophone. She felt the orgasm creeping up in her and her toes curled up as she fought against it. She wasn't ready yet.

"Noooo, Zo. I'm about to cum. You gotta stooo...Ugggggghhhh-hh!" She cried out as the wave of pleasure flowed through her. Her legs started shaking violently and Zo moaned against her inner folds, which caused a vibration that made her cum even harder. He knew what he was doing; he continued to hold her in place and suck up her juice until her shaking calmed. Kaylen felt him move upwards and she opened her eyes slowly. She was still on a high from experiencing the sensation that was still swooshing over her body. When she was able to focus her eyes, she was looking directly into Zo's eyes. The emotion that he had for her was piercing her though his eyes. It was so strong that she felt near tears and she brought her hand up to rub his face. At that moment, he pushed forward and slid his hardness directly into her. Kaylen sucked in a breath at the first push. He slid into her so effortlessly that it seemed impossible that this was their first time joining together.

Kaylen opened her legs wider and accepted him as he pushed forward into her. Zo's eyes remained locked on her face as he observed her reaction to the friction of him rubbing back and forth inside of her. Kaylen squeezed her eyes shut tightly and started rotating her hips against him. He didn't make a sound, but she could feel his breathing pick up. She opened her eyes again and saw that he had closed his as he continued moving back and forth.

What Kaylen was feeling was beyond pleasure. Her body felt something the resembled relief. She had wanted this moment for such a long time that it was almost like she had a "Waiting to Exhale" moment where she was finally able to let out that breath and release the tension that had been bottled up within her for so long. Zo's pace sped up and she felt the pang of desire ripple through her body. She arched her back and smashed her pussy up against him as if she were begging for more.

"Zo...oh...my....Gaaaa...don't stop, please!" Kaylen began rubbing up against him as he pushed down into her. Zo supported her back with one hand in order to pull her closer to him. With the other hand, he grabbed one of her nipples and squeezed it tightly between his two fingers. Kaylen gasped at the feeling that rippled through her body when he started rubbing his fingers together while squeezing her nipple in-between. Her clit swelled and pulsed against him as he continued to run his dick in and out of her. She felt the orgasm coming and her mouth fell open in anticipation. Zo wasted no time covering her mouth with his and bringing her into a deep kiss as she left the feeling overtake her. She wrapped her legs around his waist and pulled him even deeper when she felt herself getting to her peak.

"Mmmmmhmmmmm.....!" She moaned into his mouth. She wanted to scream out but he was sucking down so hard on her tongue that she couldn't part her mouth from his. Kaylen's breathing sped up as she let go and gave way to the absolute pleasure that overtook her entire mind, body, and soul. The climb was so high and she knew the coming down would be just as good. And then the doorbell rang.

Kaylen dropped her head back against the floor and groaned loudly. Zo stopped thrusting into her and they sat silently for a while as if willing the visitor to leave. The doorbell rang again and was followed by loud knocks. Kaylen sighed loudly and looked up at Zo.

"You wanna answer it?" Zo asked her. Kaylen shook her head.

"Hell, no. Can't be anyone important anyways." Kaylen said as she sat up a little and pulled him into a kiss. Zo bent down and kissed her deeply. He was still inside of her, so he began moving again and Kaylen prepared herself for what she knew would be another mind-blowing orgasm.

"Kay...are you in there?!" Kaylen's head jerked up at the sound of a voice that she knew all too well. The knocking commenced as Kaylen stared at Zo with a shocked look on her face. He smirked at her as he looked back down at her.

"Well, you want to answer it now, right?" He asked. Kaylen's mind was racing as she pulled herself up from under Zo's body and tried to gather up her clothes. Her heart was pounding so loudly in her body that she felt like it was giving her a headache. It seemed like it was making her eardrums throb. She had about three seconds to try to figure out a way to get out of this situation or at least a way to handle it, but she couldn't think of anything. She looked back at Zo. He was looking at her as if he was waiting for an answer as well, but she had none to give. So he shrugged and started collecting his clothes off the floor. More knocks at the door grabbed Kaylen's attention and she started walking towards it, but she still had no idea what to do.

What the hell is Caleb doing here?

JAZMYN

"*I*f I were a grimy ass motherfucker, where would I be?"
Jazmyn mumbled to herself as she drummed her blood red
nails against the steering wheel while sitting in the parking lot of St.
Joseph's Hospital. She tried to run through everything that Marc had
told her and Kaylen about what had happened earlier that day.

He had not mentioned Dexter returning back to a hotel, but he
had to be staying at one since Jazmyn knew he lived in New York. He
hadn't mentioned anything about whether they had met up somewhere before he invited him over to the house either. He said that
Dexter needed stitches but didn't want to go with them to the
hospital.

Hmmmm. Jazmyn continued to think of anything that could help
her. She picked up her cell and dialed the number of a person that she
knew would be able to assist.

"What up?" Dutch said once he answered the call.

"Dutch, I need you to check on something for me." Jazmyn
responded. Dutch was a part of Dom's crew. Jazmyn wasn't sure how
he did it, but he was always able to find someone. If there was a
person in Atlanta that needed to be found, he was able to do it in 24
hours. He had so many connections that it was crazy. He could get all

kinds on information, too. If there was a woman involved, he could charm the panties off her and she would be willing to hand over whatever it was that he needed.

Jazmyn never understood that part. Dutch was the ugliest mother-fucker that she had ever met in her life. He had disgusting, half-rotten teeth also. How the hell he was able the opportunity to even get in some woman's face was a mystery to her. But whatever the hell he did, it worked.

"Name?" Dutch said. His voice sounded muffled like he was chewing on something. The smacking was throwing Jazmyn off.

"Dexter. I don't have a last name."

"Tell me what you got." More smacking. Jazmyn frowned up her face in disgust.

"He may be at a hospital getting stitches for a pretty big gash on his head. Probably checked in a hotel within the last week. He was in a car accident earlier, so he may have had to rent another car. He flew into Atlanta possibly sometime this week and he is from New York..." Jazmyn's voice trailed off as she tried to think of additional information.

"That's all I need. I got it." With that Dutch hung up the phone. Jazmyn pressed the end button and turned on her car. Before she could pull out of the parking lot, her phone rang again.

"Yes?" Jazmyn said without looking at the caller id.

"Baby, I need you." Kingston said breathlessly. He was stressed and Jazmyn could hear it in his voice. Ever since the man had shown up the night before claiming to be LaShea's father, he had been on edge. Jazmyn had tried to do as much as possible to help him, but he wasn't in a place where he could hear her yet. He was in his own thoughts and instead of speaking to her; he shut himself up in the guest bedroom for the rest of the day.

"Everything ok?" Jazmyn asked as she turned out of the parking lot and headed towards the ramp to I-285.

"Yeah. I just need you home."

"On my way." Jazmyn said as she pressed her foot down harder onto the gas.

§♣

IT HAD BEEN SO LONG SINCE JAZMYN HAD BEEN ABLE TO FEEL Kingston. To smell him. To taste him or lick him. To feel him stick her toes in between his juicy lips and suck lightly until she couldn't take it anymore. Having a baby around had changed things in ways that she had never imagined. She missed being in between his legs, slipping her mouth onto his most sensitive spot as he ran his fingers through her hair and moaned. She missed coming up for air and being met with his hands lifting her up to his his face so that he could suck on her lips and place her down gently on top of him, inserting the full-ness of himself into her throbbing pussy.

There was no way to describe it other than an art. Jazmyn had been convinced when she had sex with Dom that it couldn't get any better than that. But she never loved Dom. However good a lover he was or she *thought* he was, it didn't matter because there was no emotional connection. Everything was business with him, even down to the sex. With Kingston, it was pure emotion, even from the begin-ning. The connection had been there in a way that Jazmyn had never thought she'd experience with anyone. When she started to love him, it got even better.

Here she was standing in the doorway of their bedroom, right in front of Kingston, just as naked as the way God allowed her to be when she was born. Though she carried an air of confidence every-where, it had taken her time to be comfortable standing butt-naked in front of Kingston. But he had appreciated every little imperfection on her body from day one and always made her feel beautiful.

Without saying a word, Kingston stood up from the bed and walked over to her. He grabbed her around her waist and lifted her into the air. Keeping one hand tightly around her waist, he used the other to pull one leg up and rested it on his shoulder. Jazmyn wasted no time pulling her other leg up and resting it on his other shoulder as he turned and pressed her back against the wall. She relaxed her body, using the wall and Kingston's shoulders as her support as he placed his hands up underneath her to push her up from below.

Jazmyn dropped her head and enjoyed the sensation of Kingston's wet, rough tongue licking around in her womanly folds. She crossed her legs together behind his neck and pulled him in closer.

"Mmmm...Kingston. That's so good, baby." Jazmyn moaned as she felt herself beginning to relax. She could feel the tension leaving her body. Everything about Dom, Crimson, Dexter, Alexis, Shanice's long-lost baby-daddy...all of it, was slowly leaving. Kingston pulled one hand from under her and used his thumb and middle finger to pull her lips further apart, then he stuck her tongue deep inside of her and began pulling it in and out while massaging her clit.

Oh, shit! This nigga really did need me! Jazmyn said looking down at him as he continued licking her as if he couldn't get enough. He grabbed her tightly on her ass again and the pulled her off the wall, using one hand to support her back. Then he swung her around and dropped her down onto the bed. Jazmyn barely had a chance to react before he pushed her legs back and was at it again.

"Damn, this shit feels perfect..." Jazmyn moaned as she began playing with her nipples while Kingston licked away. Suddenly he pulled his tongue out and started flicking it against her most sensitive area and it drove her wild. She pushed back in the bed and began scooting away from him. She was feeling euphoria so intense that she didn't think she could take it anymore. When Kingston sucked that piece of her into his mouth and sucked gently, Jazmyn couldn't hold it any longer and she cried out in sheer pleasure.

"Shit, Kingston, I can't take this anymore." Jazmyn said moving away from him. Kingston grabbed her tightly.

"Damn, Jaz. Stop fucking running away from me." Kingston said, his voice still muffled from being deep between her legs. The air from his speaking popping against her clit, did nothing to calm down her excitement. Just as she thought that she was able to get herself together enough to allow Kingston to continue, he began sucking again even harder and placed the tip of his finger in her ass.

What the fuck has gotten into Kingston? Jazmyn thought looking down at him, her eyes wide. She had been with many men, but this shit was new and had Jazmyn tripping. Especially when she started to enjoy it. Jazmyn continued to watch as Kingston pulled the tip of his finger out and brought it up to his mouth. He lifted up and released the tip of her clit from his mouth just long enough to suck on his finger before placing it back in her ass.

"Oh, shit, Kingston!" Jazmyn cried out again as she felt the ripples starting in her body. He was driving her insane and she did not know how to react. She was just about to cum when they heard it.

LaShea had started crying. Kingston pulled his finger out and raised his head to listen.

"Damn." He said as he stood up and ran to the bathroom to wash his face and hands. Jazmyn looked at the wetness shining all around on Kingston's face and became pissed.

"Fuck!" She yelled into one of the pillows. "Damn it, LaShae!" Kingston walked out of the bathroom and ran into the room to check in on his daughter. Jazmyn was even more frustrated than she had been before she walked in the house. Before she was stressed about work and issues with her friends. That wasn't anything she couldn't handle. This shit that just happened with Kingston was a whole different monster.

Jazmyn thought for a minute about finishing the job herself and then realized that there was no way that she would be just as satisfied when Kingston had already gotten her started. She could hear LaShea laughing in the other room as Kingston played with her.

Damn! Having a baby around just fucks up everything! Jazmyn pouted. She was not used to this. She was used to getting dick on the regular. Regular as in multiple times a day sometimes. She had heard Alexis complain often about not liking to have sex all the time, but that was not Jazmyn's problem. In her mind, if you didn't always want it then something wasn't being done right.

Jazmyn heard her phone ring and she rolled over out of the bed then tiptoed out of the room. She walked into the living room and grabbed the phone just in time to catch the call before going to voicemail.

"What you got?" She said.

"An address." Jazmyn looked around for something to write with.

"Can you text it to me?"

"Naw, Jay. You know I don't do that shit. You tryna get me caught up?" Dutch said. Jazmyn groaned and walked over into the kitchen. She began moving stuff around looking for a pen and anything that she could write with.

"Give me the address." She said once she found a notebook inside of a drawer of one of the kitchen counters.

"Aight. Nigga full name is Dexter Malcolm. Address is 400 West Peachtree Str..."

"Hold up...he's at *Twelve?*" As soon as she said it, she heard dead air so she knew Dutch had hung up. She also knew she was right.

Fuck! Everybody in the world knows who the hell I am at Twelve! *How the hell am I about to pull this off?* Jazmyn groaned as she sunk down in a seat just outside the kitchen. She tossed the notebook over onto a desk next to her and thought about what her next moves should be.

"Everything fine?" Kingston started walking towards her with a confused look on his face. "You seem like something is wrong."

"Where is LaShae?" Jazmyn asked. Something was wrong. She was in the middle of tense situations and needed to find a way to get rid of the built up anxiety.

"I put her back to sleep." As soon as the words left his mouth, Jazmyn jumped up and walked over to Kingston. She gave him a deep kiss and pulled at the buckle of the jeans he was wearing. They fell easily to the floor as Jazmyn explored his mouth with her tongue. Kingston wrapped his arms around her pulled her close.

Enough of this sweet shit. Jazmyn thought as she pushed him away. With the day that she'd had, she was ready to play a little rough. She turned around and bent down low to the floor, tooting her ass into the air. Kingston knew what she wanted and he was ready to please her. He pulled his dick out of the flap in his boxers then grabbed onto the side of her waist. Jazmyn inhaled sharply when she felt him push forcefully in the first time. Kingston usually slid it in slowly, but apparently he needed to relieve just as much stress as she did.

Jazmyn moaned as she felt him continue to ram into her. The force of his pumps nearly propelled her across the room and into the wall, but he was holding onto her so tightly that even if she lost her footing, Kingston would just continue right on while her feet dangled in the air.

"*Shit!* Kingston….mmmhmmm…you must have missed the fuck outta me!" Jazmyn said between pumps.

"You have no idea." Kingston said as he pulled out all the way. He ushered her over to the sofa and then pulled off his shirt before sitting down. Jazmyn climbed on top of him, facing him, and the wrapped her legs around behind him so that he could get in even deeper. Then she began grinding her ass on him and bouncing as hard as she could. Kingston grabbed on to her back and pulled her in close as he pushed up from below, popping her further and further in the air.

Yes, God! This is exactly what I needed today. Finally! Jazmyn thought to herself. The friction of her nipple rubbing up against his chest as she moved made her get wetter and wetter. Jazmyn began grinding her pussy harder as she clutched on to the back of Kingston's neck. The stickiness that she felt on her thighs turned her on and she wanted more of him. She bent down and bit on his neck and it made Kingston moan in ecstasy. Jazmyn felt herself about to cum and she started riding him faster. She gritted her teeth and held her breath once she felt the sensation rising up through her. Kingston held her tight and continued pumping upwards since he could tell that she was at her peak.

"Shit, Kingston!" Jazmyn squeezed her eyes closed and yelled out as she felt the orgasm run through her. She arched her back and moaned as the feeling ran its course from the tips of her toes, up through every follicle on the top of her head. When she finally opened her eyes, Kingston was looking right into them.

"You good, Jaz?"

"Hell, yeah. I'm real good, baby." She responded with a smile.

"Alright then." Kingston stood up, still holding Jazmyn on his lap. He walked over to the dining room table and laid her on top of it. Jazmyn grew excited and her nipples hardened, exposing her feelings. Kingston bent down and kissed her gently on her lips, then move forward suddenly at the same time. He pulled back then pushed her legs up so that they were open wide and her knees were pushed up almost to her shoulders. He started pumping and playing inside of her at the same time. Jazmyn couldn't take it and it drove her absolutely crazy. The ferocious pumping mixed with the thumping, rubbing and flicking that he was doing on her clitoris was driving her to ecstasy all over again. He sucked on his fingers, making sure to leave them nice and moist before continuing to run them up, down and all around her treasure box.

Jazmyn squeezed her eyes shut when she felt Kingston tense up and the pumps became faster and faster. She knew he was about to cum and she was about to right along with him.

"Fuck, Jaz....damn....this shit is....so....good!" Kingston said as he jammed himself deep inside her. One final thrust and Jazmyn's cries mixed with Kingston's moans as they arrived at their ultimate pleasure together. Kingston fell over on top of her for a moment to catch his breath. Jazmyn wrapped her arms around him and held him. They had been rough with each other before, but this time the intensity was at an all-time high and Jazmyn knew it was because of everything that was going on.

Kingston sat up and pulled out of her and picked her up off the table. He carried her in his arms into the room as she laid her head against his chest. The smell of him was something that stayed with her even when they weren't together. When he was married to Shanice, Jazmyn would stay asleep in the hotel appreciating the fact that she could still smell his cologne and imagine that he was there with her. Now she was able to do that every day and the happiness that she'd felt was beyond anything she could have imagined for herself.

Kingston laid her down on the bed and fell down beside her. She snuggled close to him as he pulled her into his arms and nestled his nose inside of her hair. Jazmyn closed her eyes and exhaled deeply, ready to enjoy a nice nap with her man. But LaShea wasn't having it. Jazmyn felt Kingston tense up when they heard the little girl's cries. Suddenly Kingston burst out laughing.

What's so damn funny? Jazmyn thought as she turned to look at him. Kingston continued laughing to the point that Jazmyn could no longer hold it in anymore and she began to laugh to. Finally, he pulled away and stepped out of the bed.

"This shit is different for us, huh?" Kingston said as he started pulling on pants that had been lying on a chair in the room.

"Yeah this shit is definitely different." Jazmyn said as she watched him walk out of the door to comfort LaShea.

ALEXIS

"*A*lexis, are you sure you will be fine? You don't want me to wait for you?" Alexis looked at Duchess with utter shock and surprise. It wasn't like her to try to be so motherly.

"No, Duchess. I will be fine. I hope that Marc will be home soon anyways." Alexis looked at her her watch as she started to gather her things to get out of the car. It was only about six o'clock. It had been a long day. The day's events had made it seem like it should have been late at night…or even another day, but here it was; only dinner time.

"Well, lock up and be safe. I can't believe that he just left like that." Duchess searched Alexis' face as she tried to judge whether or not Alexis had any information to share on her husband's whereabouts. Finally she sighed and sat back in her seat. "Ok, Alexis. Well, I will give you a call a little later to check on you. I need to check on your father now anyways." Alexis took this as her cue to go ahead and leave. She didn't want to get in the middle of the Duchess checking in on her "life line."

"Ok. Later." Alexis mumbled as she slammed the door behind her. She was barely to the front door before Duchess started speeding off down the winding driveway.

That motherly shit never lasts long, Alexis thought to herself as she opened the door. She closed the door behind her and dropped her keys on the side table by the door after locking up. Her next action was to get over to the bar and pour herself a glass full of Courvoisier. No ice, because there was none needed. After the day that she'd had, she just wanted to feel the warm liquid travel down within her.

Five glasses later, Alexis was feeling pretty good. The room was swirling around her, but she was no longer sad about what happened earlier with Dexter. The whole ordeal actually seemed quite funny when she thought about the way that his body collapsed under the force of the vase that she smashed over his head.

"Shit, I wish I could do that all over again." Alexis thought as she sipped more of her drink. She glanced at her cellphone and picked it up. She knew that she probably shouldn't have been making calls in her current state, but she decided that she needed to call to check on Marc. She had not seen him since he walked out of her room at the hospital and that had been hours earlier.

"The person you have dialed cannot come to the ph..." Alexis groaned and press the button to end the call. She tossed the phone down beside her on the bed and leaned backwards over it allowing her head to hang upside down and her hair to swoop the floor. She jerked back upwards when she heard a knock at the door. She picked up her cellphone and looked at the time.

It's 12:20...who is here at this time of night? Alexis thought as she rose up from the bed and started creeping to the door. There wasn't a gun in the house, so once she got down the stairs she ran over to the kitchen and grabbed a butcher knife. She tucked it close to her body and tiptoed to the door. She peeked through the peephole. Standing on the other side of the door was a man that she recognized as one of Marc's business partners. He had been to the house a few times in the past, but it had been a while. Why he was showing up here so late at night was a mystery though.

"Hi....uh...Marc isn't here!" Alexis said through the door. She didn't want to be rude, but she didn't trust the man enough to open the door. Marc's business partner or not, he looked pretty shady to her at the moment. She pressed her eye closer to the peephole to look at the man closer. He was Caucasian, but still kind of dark, like Marc. He had most of his jet black hair covered under a black skull cap. He was wearing a black long-sleeve shirt with black jeans. He was casual, but still very well put together.

"Ok...you the wife, huh? Well, he told me to meet him here." Alexis paused as she tried to think of what to do next. Marc wasn't here and she was not about to let this man in the house.

"Hold on a minute!" She said before turning around and running over to the living room to grab one of the landline phones. She pecked in Marc's number quickly and then waited as it rang.

"Lexi. Is there a problem?" Alexis paused at Marc's tone. She was used to him sounding soft and gentle with her. His voice always held so much care when he spoke to her. At this moment, she felt something different although he had barely spoke a few words. He sounded commanding, forceful and in charge. Almost like she had interrupted a business meeting that he had with the President of the United States. Hell, *he* sounded as if he was POTUS himself. Alexis frowned up her eyebrows at his tone as she immediately began to sober up.

"Um...there is a man at the door. He says you were supposed to meet with him." Alexis stammered as she looked back to the door.

"Yes. I am coming down the drive now. See you soon." Marc disconnected the line and Alexis sat in place for a minute holding the phone as she tried to process what had just happened. She glanced towards the front door when she heard the soft growl of a car engine in the yard, which alerted her to the fact that Marc had pulled up. Alexis walked over to the door and looked out the peephole. She saw the man walk over as Marc got out of the car and they spoke to each other too low for her to hear through the door. She backed away and ran over to sit on the sofa when she saw that they were about to enter the house. As the door unlocked and swung open, Alexis pretended to be flipping through a magazine.

"Hi Marc," Alexis said as she looked up into his eyes. He didn't say anything back, but he did acknowledge her presence with a nod and then ushered his guest over to his office. Alexis was perplexed. He didn't even ask how she was since leaving the hospital. Truthfully, she wasn't feeling bad at all, but he still was expected to ask or be concerned. However, he wasn't. Alexis poked her lip out and pouted a little.

I guess it serves me right for acting evil the past few months when he actually was concerned. Alexis watched as the two men headed over to his office in silence. Something wasn't right about the looks on their faces. They seemed extremely serious and secretive. Alexis' curiosity was peeked. As soon as they entered Marc's office and closed the door behind them, she slammed the magazine down beside her and jumped off the couch. She tip-toed over to the door and pressed her ear against it. Holding her breath, she listened intently and prayed that no one would come out the room while she was standing there eaves-dropping.

"Did you get it?" That was Marc. Alexis squinted her eyes as she tried to think about what he could possibly been referring to.

"Yeah, I got an address. That all you wanted?" The man asked Marc. Alexis heard some ruffling, like the sound of papers being sifted through.

"Give it here." Marc commanded. His voice was all business. Demanding and intimidating. He was obviously the one in charge. Alexis heard some ruffling and figured it was the man searching for something to hand over to Marc.

"Is this a hit? You sure you don't need me to handle something for you, boss?" The man asked.

Boss? Alexis asked herself with a puzzled look on her face. *Why is he calling him boss like that?* It didn't sound like the way that someone says "boss" during casual conversation. This man was speaking as if Marc really was the boss! His tone was pure respect and Marc was speaking as his commander in chief.

What the fuck is going on? Alexis thought to herself. She scratched the top of her head as she tried to sort out what was going on in her home. Her thoughts were interrupted when the shrill sound of her cellphone ringer began to sound through the quiet.

"Oh, shiiii...." Alexis whispered as she tried to dart quickly away from the door and silence her phone at the same time. She rounded the corner away from Marc's office right before she heard the door swing open.

"That you, Lex?" Marc's deep voice vibrated through the hall as Alexis continued tipping up the stairs. Alexis looked down at the screen of her phone and saw that it was Vanessa calling.

Damn it, Vanessa! Perfect time for you to try to be a sister!

"Yes?" Alexis whispered as she picked up the phone. She returned to her normal volume of speaking once she made it to her bedroom and sat down on the bed. "Vanessa...what is it?"

"Lexi...wait, first, are you ok?" Alexis rolled her eyes.

I know this chick ain't interrupting my snooping just to check on my health status.

"Yes, I'm fine. That's all you wanted?" Alexis snapped. She knew she was being rude, but she was annoyed that Vanessa's call had interrupted her from listening to Marc's conversation and had probably busted her.

"No. I just wanted your advice about something. I'm thinking about dating again and..." Vanessa started.

"Yeah, I know you told me. But you still love Ty and you are having a hard time moving on." Alexis rushed her as she stood up from the bed and walked out of her bedroom. She thought that she had heard a noise and peeked over the ledge of the balcony to see what was going on. As she leaned over, she looked eye to eye right into Marc's blue eyes. He was looking at her sternly and the intensity of his gaze made Alexis pull back quickly away from the stairs. Seconds later, she heard his heavy footsteps on the steps of the stairs.

"Yes, Lex, but I wanted to talk to you about something else, too...." Vanessa started. Alexis looked to her left and saw Marc walking towards where she stood.

"Uh...Vanessa, I need to call you back, ok?"

"Yeah, but Lex, I need to..." Alexis pressed the end button on the phone before Vanessa could finish.

She will understand.

"Lexi, everything ok with you?" Marc said giving her a hard look. Alexis felt like he was looking into her soul. He was staring at her so hard that she almost felt a little intimidated. She felt herself shrinking away from his gaze as she began to feel like a little afraid of the new Marc. He must have noticed her reaction to him because his expression changed to one of care and concern. It was more of what Alexis was used to seeing.

"Is everything ok?" Marc repeated as he walked up close to her and pulled her into a hug. Alexis allowed him to hold her and she returned his embrace.

"You weren't listening at the door, right?" Marc asked as he pulled back to look her in the eyes. Alexis hurriedly shook her head 'no'. Marc stared at her for a while without saying a word.

"Ok. Well, I have to go for a little bit for business. I may be back in the morning." Marc said before pulling her into a forehead kiss.

"Where do you have to go?" Alexis asked nervously. She remembered what she had told him earlier concerning Dexter. He seemed so angry when he left, but now he was calm, collected and in charge. She felt like something was brewing between him and this "business partner," but he wasn't letting out any information.

"I may be back in the morning. Lock up everything. Call me if you need me." Marc said before turning around to head down the stairs and towards the front door. The man that had been in the office with him was already waiting outside. Alexis jogged down the stairs and to the window to peep outside. She watched as the two men spoke for a short while before jumping into separate cars and speeding off down the driveway. Something was going on and Alexis knew she had to find out.

KAYLEN

aylen was at a loss for words as she looked at Caleb's confused stare. She was positive that he was wondering why she hadn't invited him in yet...it was a reasonable question since he was her fiancé and she was standing at the door, blocking his entrance into her home. But she had no idea what to say to him about it.

"Umm...Caleb. Baby, what are you doing here? I just spoke to you this morning." Kaylen said as she tried to quickly run all the possible scenarios through her mind. None of them seemed to go well for her.

Damn it!

"Well I thought that the situation with Tiffany should be spoke about in person, so I hopped on the next fli....Wait, Kay...why am I still standing out here? And whose car is that?" Caleb asked as he used his thumb to point behind him at Zo's black Porsche. Kaylen paused before answering and she felt the tell-tell signs of guilt creeping up onto her face. Caleb noticed it, too, and she watched as his eyes finally looked over her. His facial expression changed as he finally noticed her disheveled appearance. Her hair was all over her head and her clothes were thrown on in a manner that had to scream: "I've just been having the time of my life rolling around having the best sex in the…"

"It's my car. I was just leaving. Kay…how about we finish studying later?" Kaylen turned around to look at Zo as he pulled the door open wide enough to scoot pass her. He was holding her anatomy book in his hand.

"Uh….yeah. I will call you." Kaylen said looking up at Caleb. He did not seem convinced that Zo was only there to study, but he didn't look angry anymore either.

"Hey, I'm Zo. I'm just leaving." Zo said extending his hand out to Caleb. Kaylen looked at Zo and noticed that although he was trying to keep a straight face, there was obvious humor in his eyes. He even had a smirk forming at the sides of his mouth. Kaylen couldn't blame him…the whole situation was a mess. Just ten minutes ago, he was knee deep in her pussy and now here he was about to shake hands with her fiancé. Her scent was still on his breath. If this wasn't happening to her, it would be hilarious and wonderful drama.

"I'm Caleb. Kaylen's fiancé." Caleb said giving Zo a stern look. He reached out to him and shook his hand. Kaylen watched as the two men eyed each other silently. A lot was being said although they weren't talking.

"So…um, bye Zo. I will call you. Caleb, you want to come in?" Kaylen said moving out of the way to allow Caleb to enter. Caleb and Zo gave each other a final hard stare down before Caleb started to walk into the house.

"Yeah, baby. I've been missing you and I'm ready to show you how much." Caleb said loud enough for Zo to hear as he walked in. Kaylen's eyes shot towards Zo when she heard him chuckle quietly. He caught her look and tried to disguise it as a cough which made Kaylen smile despite her current situation. Her smile stayed until she turned around and closed the door behind her. The look of suspicion on Caleb's face wiped the smile off of her face about as fast as Zo was able to put it there.

"Studying, huh?" Caleb asked. Kaylen neither affirmed nor denied his question. "I don't remember him being a student at Emory." Kaylen continued to look at him for a second before letting her eyes look across the living room. Thankfully, it looked like Zo had made everything appear normal again before he left. She made a mental note to thank him for that.

"So you came here to talk about Tiffany?" Kaylen asked crossing her arms in front of her and raising one eyebrow. She knew that Caleb would probably bring up the Zo situation again at some point, but she wasn't about to allow him to make this about her just yet.

"I did. Let's sit down." Caleb said pointing to one of the chairs near him.

"I'm good." Kaylen said still standing with her arms crossed.

"Ok, fine," He sighed as he sat down. He sat on the edge of the chair and leaned up to place his elbows on his knees. He looked at her for a minute before rubbing his face with his hands and then letting out another long and heavy sigh.

"Tiffany and I dated back when I was a professor at Emory. It started before I met you, but we did mess around a little after, too." Caleb paused for a minute as he tried to collect his words before continuing. "One day, I broke it off with her. She became too posses- sive. In the beginning she knew her place in my life. I wasn't ready to commit to anyone. Then something changed and all of a sudden she wanted more. She would go through my phone and text other women I was dealing with." Kaylen nodded a little when he said that. Tiffany hadn't ever texted her, but she had confronted her in person one day.

That must have been around the time this bitch decided to go crazy....

"Anyways, I ended things with her and she dropped out of the medical program. About two months later, I got a call from her crazy ass sister, Tameka, saying that I wasn't just gonna avoid my responsi- bilities and that Tiffany didn't make the baby alone." Caleb frowned up his face as he continued. "I didn't know what the hell she was talking about. I had no idea that she was pregnant, but apparently Tiffany had been telling her family that I left her when I found out she was pregnant. I went to see her and Candace had already been born." Caleb threw his hands up in the air and shrugged.

"Well, did you get a paternity test?" Kaylen asked.

Bitches fake a baby all the time and have some poor soul paying out the ass for a baby that ain't even theirs.

"I did. Candace is mine." Now Kaylen had to take a seat. She walked over and sat down across from Caleb.

"How old is she?" Kaylen asked. She was trying not to appear too upset. She wasn't upset about the baby; she was upset that the baby was attached to a bitch like Tiffany. That girl was sure to be the baby mama from hell.

"She will be two in six months." Kaylen did the calculations in her mind. Everything added up to match his story.

"Why didn't you tell me about it?" Caleb shrugged again.

"I didn't know how to do it." They sat in silence for a moment longer. Kaylen was trying to figure out what was going on with her life. On one hand, she had a man who seemed like he genuinely cared for her and he had even asked her to marry him. So what he had a child from a Grade A Bitch...Kaylen had her own skeletons in the closet and a handful and a half of a mistakes that Caleb knew nothing about. On the other hand, there was Zo. They hadn't had the opportunity to pursue a relationship and Kaylen really wanted to know what would happen with that. It wasn't fair to Caleb to get married to him when she still wanted Zo.

Hell, I was just having sex with the nigga almost right where Caleb has his feet! Embarrassment and guilt came upon her as she started to remember what exactly she had been doing when Caleb had knocked on the door. She really wasn't in a position to pass judgment right now. But she still had some questions.

"When's the last time you fucked around with her?" Kaylen asked, still trying to hold on to her "attitude." She wasn't upset, but she felt like she needed to keep the attitude to throw off her own feelings of guilt.

"Not since we've been together officially." Caleb said quickly.

"When was the last time?" Kaylen asked again.

"That night that I called you and said I wanted to see you and make it official. I had just left her place and she was acting crazy again. I decided then that I was tired of that kind of life. I wanted something stable and I wanted to do that with you." Kaylen thought a minute about picking a fight about the fact that it took Tiffany acting crazy for him to realize that, but she decided not to. She started to lie back in her seat when she heard someone banging at the door.

What the fu....I'm so done with people just showing up over here! Kaylen thought to herself as she frowned and stood up to walk over to the door.

"Expecting someone?" Caleb asked her.

"Not at all..." Kaylen grumbled under her breath. She was not in the mood for any more drama and from the banging at the door, it seemed like that's what she was about to get. Kaylen walked over to the door and looked out the peephole.

"Oh, hell no!" She said out loud before hastily unlocking the door and swinging it open.

"The fuck you doing over here, bitch? You lost your damn mind or something?" Kaylen said as she looked at Tiffany. The girl looked like five day old road-kill. Kaylen knew that she wasn't dressed her best, but she was in her own home. Tiffany actually had the audacity to step out her house looking like something that was stuck at the bottom of a trashcan. Her weave was matted and tossed in a loose ponytail. She had on far too much make-up and her foundation wasn't even the right color for her complexion. She was a brown color and she looked like she was wearing something meant for Raven Simone. She had outlined her olive-shaped eyes with a thick line of black eyeliner and she had on the reddish lipstick on the shelf. Kaylen curled her lip up as she looked at her.

What did Caleb see in this hoe?

"Get out of my way. I know he in here! I see his car right there and I need to speak with him about *our* daughter!" Tiffany proceeded to move as if she was about to walk into the house and Kaylen pushed her back.

"I know your nasty ass don't think that you're about to walk your slimy self up into my house! The fuck wrong with you?" Kaylen yelled. She heard movement behind her and knew that Caleb must have been walking up to the door. Tiffany rolled her eyes at Kaylen and then shifted them to Caleb.

"There you are! What you can't answer my calls now? You don't think you need to see bout your daughter?" Tiffany twirled her neck and waved her finger in the air as she talked to Caleb. Kaylen shook her head as she looked at her with pity. Tiffany used to be one of the top students in their medical program. Now she was nothing but a hood-ass, ratchet-ass babymama still stuck on her babydaddy's dick.

"What are you doing here, Tiff? What you been staking out the house or something?" Caleb asked.

"She must've been because it look like the bitch ain't bathed in weeks!" Kaylen said looking Tiffany up and down.

"Kay, let me handle this real quick." Caleb said lowly. Kaylen looked at him like he was crazy.

"That's right! Take your ass in the house while us *grown folks* handle *our* business!" Tiffany said with a smug look on her face. Kaylen noticed some of her neighbors peeking out of their doors and window to observe the disturbance to the, otherwise, very quiet street, but she didn't care.

"Hell to the *fuck* no! You are on my motherfuckin' property. If you want to talk to this piece of trash, Caleb, you need to take her ass to the street. Her hoe ass should be used to walking up and down the street looking for dick anyways." Kaylen hissed. She felt satisfied when she saw Caleb shrug after Tiffany gave him a hard look. There was nothing he could do. This townhouse was in Kaylen's name and hers alone.

"Get the hell on. I'm waiting..." Kaylen said folding her arms in front of her and tapping her foot on the ground. Tiffany groaned loudly before turning to walk to the curb. Caleb followed behind her. Kaylen laughed to herself.

This bitch is thirsty as hell, because there is no way in the world that I would talk to a nigga on the curb. I would rather have jumped my ass in my car and just left.

"And don't bring your ass back on my property either!" Kaylen said right before she stepped back in the house and slammed the door behind her.

JAZMYN

"Shit!" This was not how this was supposed to go down. Of all the places that Dexter could be, he had to be staying at *Twelve*. The hotel that Kingston and her frequented when Shanice was alive. Everyone from the valet to the bellboy to the manager who was only there once a week knew exactly who she was by name. Jazmyn looked over in her passenger seat and grabbed up the jacket, shades, and the hat that she'd brought with her. It wasn't a great disguise, but anything more would raise alarms. The shades weren't a big deal although it was so late in the night. Celebrities frequented this hotel, so they would probably assume that she was one of them, trying to creep in quietly without being noticed.

Jazmyn sighed and threw the shades on her face, placed the coat around her arms and then tugged the hat over her hair.

If this goes wrong, I will have a lot more people on my hit list to deal with, Jazmyn thought to herself as she walked to the entrance of the hotel. Once she walked in, she immediately lost focus. Her thoughts went to the last time she was here with Kingston. It was the day that she had killed Shanice. He had called her to tell her that he had left Shanice for good and he asked her to meet him here. Jazmyn remembered the moment that she walked through the doors, the first face that she was

119

Kingston's. He was so eager to see her that he was waiting on the bottom floor of the hotel with tears in his eyes. Jazmyn immediately grew worried that someone had already contacting him about Shanice, but that wasn't the case at all.

"Kingston, are you ok, baby?" Jazmyn had said as she walked over to him slowly. She was unsure what to expect. The guilt of what she had done was bottled up in her for the time being, but she could feel it eating away at her insides like acid. She didn't know how long she could hold it in before it would start to bleed through onto her face. Kingston had always been great at deciphering the emotions that her face conveyed, whether she had wanted him to or not. There would have been no way to hide it once the guilt showed.

"Yes, Jaz. I'm just so happy that you came." Kingston had replied to her. He pulled her into his arms and she exhaled. She was at peace when they were together. Her life was turmoil and chaos everywhere else, but Kingston brought her balance and peace. She couldn't survive...couldn't live if it weren't for him.

Now here she was. Not even two hours after she was experiencing pure bliss and satisfaction in his arms, she was about to summon her inner Lady Death and payback someone who deeply deserved what was coming to him.

And payback will be a motherfucker, Jazmyn thought to herself. Jazmyn looked at the reservation counter at the employees working. She saw a small blond woman, fairly young and petite at the counter. She was fussing with her hair and biting her lip. She was new because Jazmyn had never seen her before and from the looks of it, she was frustrated and having a hard time with something.

Bingo. Jazmyn walked over to the counter in a hurry and tried to lay on her best "damsel in distress" act.

"Hi, excuse me. My husband told me to meet him here. His name is Dexter Malcolm. Someone stole my purse and I don't have my phone, money or anything! I can't believe this! My God, I'm so scared. Can you please tell me which room my husband is in?" Jazmyn prayed silently that her bad acting would work. God would be mad at her in a minute, so she wasn't too sure that he would answer this prayer.

"Sure, ma'am. Oh my God, I'm so, so sorry to hear that! Are you ok?" Jazmyn would have felt bad for the girl if it wasn't so damn funny. The young girl's eyes were wide and her mouth was stretched open as far as it could go. But the funny thing to Jazmyn was that her mouth leaned a little to one side. Her expression read "This is the *last fucking thing I need right now!*" Jazmyn tried to stifle her laughter as best as she could and she continued on.

"No, I don't need anything but my husband. Can you please tell me which room he is in?" Jazmyn tried to continue sounding as distressed as possible, but it was hard because the situation was beginning to be a little amusing.

"Sure! He is in room 803." Jazmyn turned and started walking towards the elevators. "Mrs. Malcolm, do you need a key?" Jazmyn stopped and tried to keep down the smile that was teasing her lips.

This is going to be easier than I thought.

"Yes, that would be so nice. Thank you so much. I will write a letter to the manager about how much of a help that you were today." The girl smiled and Jazmyn almost felt bad that she would probably be fired by tomorrow.

Jazmyn walked over to the elevators quickly. She was still afraid that she would see someone that she knew. There had been plenty of times that she and Kingston had spent a lot of money requesting room service and extra luxury items within this hotel. They were also pretty big tippers so most of the staff knew them when they saw them and knew to look out for them. Jazmyn said a silent prayer that in the months they had been away from the hotel, the staff had forgotten them.

"Ms. Jazmyn?" Jazmyn cringed inwardly as she heard the voice of one of the bellboys that she'd become acquainted with since coming here with Kingston.

I guess God's not going to answer my prayers twice in one day. Damn it! Jazmyn fought the urge to turn around and walk right out of the building. Instead she ignored the young man and jumped onto the elevator as soon as it opened. She smashed her finger against the button for the eighth floor and then pushed the other button to close the doors. This was becoming a horribly put together plan. And that made sense because it wasn't thought out at all. Jazmyn had reacted based on her emotion and that was something that Crimson had told her never to do. You should never act on emotion because then your vision is too fucked up to see all the details. Jazmyn exhaled as the elevator doors opened. She walked off the elevator slowly as she felt doubt creeping up in her. But then she started to remember why she was here in the first place.

Jaz, this man violated your friend. Your family. You have killed mother-fuckers for less. Time to shake the extra off and do what you have to do. That was all the pep talk that Jazmyn needed. She noted the sign on the wall that told her which way room 803 was and she turned the corner ready to do what she needed to do. She reached into the pocket of the coat and checked to make sure that the tools she needed were rolled up in the pretend make-up bag disguise that she used; then she reached back behind her to make sure her knife was in place. She felt the doubt being replaced by excitement. This was about to be the most fun that she'd had since....well, since Shanice.

Jazmyn slipped the key card into the door and smirked when she heard the satisfying click that let her know she could enter. The last time she had checked with Dutch, he was able to confirm that Dexter's cellphone GPS signal was still indicating that he was at the hotel, so Jazmyn hoped like hell there would be no surprises. She crept into the room and slowly closed the door behind her as quietly as she could. She winced when she heard the soft click of the door behind her.

The room was so quiet that the sound was magnified a little louder than normal. The room was also dark, but there was a little light shining through from the window so Jazmyn was able to make out a few things in the room. She walked in further and she could see a body lying in the middle of the King-sized bed in the room. It was a male, so she knew it had to be Dexter. Jazmyn pulled out the syringe that was in her pocket. It was Pavulon, a paralyzing agent, and she had enough of it handy to paralyze a baby elephant. As soon as she got close enough to confirm that the person on the bed was indeed

Dexter, she shoved the tip of the syringe deep into his side and tapped the top lightly enough to push about half of the liquid into him. Then she waited about three minutes for it to take effect.

Now it's time to get to business. Jazmyn turned on the small lamp next to the bed as she began to get excited. But her excitement was short-lived once she took a second look at Dexter. Jazmyn's mouth fell open and she gasped loudly at the sight.

Dexter was lying on the bed with his mouth open, locked in an "O" formation. He had a bullet-hole going cleanly through the front of his head straight to the back. His eyes were open as well and still held the last emotion that he must have felt before meeting his maker: Fear.

Jazmyn covered her mouth as she tried to understand what had occurred. She came to this hotel to kill Dexter, but he was now already dead.

Who would have killed him? Who in Atlanta wanted him dead? No one knew that he was the one that had raped Alexis except....

Vanessa? Jazmyn scrunched up her face at the thought. That was highly unlikely. She had known about Dexter for a while so it didn't make sense that she waited all this time to kill him.

Unless she had been waiting for the perfect opportunity! Or maybe she got Dom and Crimson to do it for her. Jazmyn thought to herself. Either way, she knew that it was time for her to get out of the room. Jazmyn broke off the tip of the syringe and tossed it in the trash before placing the rest of it into her pocket. Then she walked casually out of the room. Once she was on the first floor, she walked briskly pass the young woman who had helped her earlier. She still seemed stressed and flustered so she didn't even notice Jazmyn leave. Since Dexter had already been dead, the girl may just be able to salvage her job since the death occurred prior to her allowing Jazmyn entrance.

Who knows? All I know is that I have a few phone calls to make about this.

"Where are you?" Jazmyn asked gruffly. She was not in the mood for pleasantries and couldn't care less about being nice. Something was going on behind the scenes and she needed to know what. She was out of the loop in the worst way and had almost stumbled upon something that could have ruined her once again. She had no idea that Vanessa was planning on having someone from Dom's team kill Dexter. The situation could have gotten ugly if she had walked in there at the wrong time carrying everything that she had on her.

"In the bed. Why…what's going on?" Vanessa sounded like she had been in the middle of sleeping, but Jazmyn wasn't convinced. It was already apparent that the girl could put on a hell of a show. This little acting game she was playing now couldn't be that hard.

"Get your ass up. I need you to meet me now and don't make me wait." Jazmyn sneered.

I knew not to fuck around with this girl when I saw her standing outside of my door. I should have just left her ass standing there looking lost.

"What? It's the middle of the ni…."

"You either bring your ass over to my house within the hour, or I'm coming to your parent's crib to get you. Choose one." Jazmyn said before hanging up. She mashed the gas on her fire red Audi and turned to get onto I-75 and head to her condo.

About ten minutes after Jazmyn had arrived home, she heard a knock on her door.

"Damn. She got here quick…Must have known that I meant business." Jazmyn dropped her Essence magazine down on her coffee table and walked over to the door. She knew it was Vanessa, so she didn't bother looking through the peephole. Once she opened the door, she knew that was a mistake.

"Expecting us?" Crimson asked with a smile. Dom nodded his greeting at Jazmyn before walking in past her like he owned the place. Crimson followed behind him and stopped only to pat Jazmyn on the shoulder before walking pass her. Jazmyn sighed quietly and was about to close the door when she saw another person enter the doorway. He was standing on the side of the entrance to the door, so Jazmyn hadn't seen him at first. He looked vaguely familiar, but she couldn't place his name. She paused for a minute as she tried to figure out what he was doing standing in front of her condo.

"Can I help you?" Jazmyn asked him, giving him a once over. He was very attractive; dark-skin tone, perfectly laid goatee and the prettiest light brown eyes that she had ever seen. She googled at Kingston's eyes on a daily basis, but it was something about the way his brown eyes set against his deep chocolate brown skin that made her take in a breath. He was dress impeccably in a gold and white Versace button-up with Versace jeans that had gold stitching and a gold and white embroidery, along with and gold Versace sneakers. He was "hood chic" and it was so sexy. But Jazmyn still needed answers as to why he was standing in front of her home.

"Oh...he's with us. Don't mind her boss, she ain't know." Dom said from behind her. Jazmyn moved out of the way to let the man enter. He looked over his shoulder quickly before walking in. Jazmyn turned her back to him to push the door closed; once she turned back around, she was looking directly in his eyes. She stopped for a second in alarm as well as admiration of how sexy they were before she noticed his outstretched hand.

"I wanted to introduce myself. I'm Ty." He said giving her a firm look. Jazmyn's mouth dropped open for the second time in the matter of a few hours.

Oh...my...God. This is Ty? It can't be...everyone said he was dead. What the hell?

"I guess you've heard of me?" Ty said raising one eyebrow and taking back his hand. He stuffed it into his pocket and then ran his other hand over the top of his head. Jazmyn struggled to collect herself.

"Yes...I have. But, why are you..." Jazmyn started.

"That's what we have come to discuss." Crimson chimed in. She motioned to the chair across from her and Jazmyn followed her unspoken order to sit down. Ty followed behind Jazmyn at a slower pace. Once Jazmyn sat down, she was able to see why. He walked with a limp. It wasn't a huge limp, and it wasn't incredibly noticeable, but she was trained to detect even the smallest of things so she noticed it right away.

"You already know the story of Ty. He is the boss. He's the one that united *The Disciples* and made us who we are. Before him, we were just the *2-Fiyah* crew and *The Family*, but after what everyone believes to be his "death," the two gangs united as one under his memory and we became who we are today. Anyways, it's obvious that the boss survived...he's a real G. Bullets can't touch 'em." Dom's face glowed. Jazmyn blinked with amazement. She had never seen Dom in such a great mood. He was like a little kid who had just been promised a trip to Disney. All smiles and white teeth. It was incredulous.

"Anyways," Crimson interrupted giving Dom a sideways look. She must have noticed that Dom was getting too caught up in the story and, as typical with her, she was ready to get down to business. "The boss needs someone with your skill to join him in Miami. He's making some heavy moves and we need people down there that we can trust." Jazmyn struggled not to let her mouth drop open again.

I will be damned if my mouth drop open for the third time tonight. I fucking hate surprises! Jazmyn looked over to Ty who had been sitting in the seat quietly with his eyes closed. He looked rather relaxed, but overall incredibly friendly and charming. He didn't seem anything like the stories that she'd heard about him. Sure, he looked like there was more to him than meets the eyes. It was obvious that he had an air of confidence and an authoritative feel about him, but he seemed more approachable and kind than she had thought he would be. He suddenly opened his eyes and sat up in the seat.

"It's like this." He paused for a minute. "I'm poised and ready to take over the entire area, but I got a few hiccups in the plan. I need someone that I can trust with me down there. Crimson needs to stay here. We have a few others, but Dom and Crim said that you were the best choice to help me lead that group. Alright?" Jazmyn looked at all of the eyes staring at her. Although he had said it as a question, she knew it wasn't. She also now understood what was going on. Dom and Crimson hadn't just "nominated" her for the job because she was loyal and she was one of the best. They wanted her to go in order to distance her from Kingston. Jazmyn sat back in her seat. Her head hurt...she knew what she was being asked to do, but she couldn't do it. Kingston already had too much going on.

"When?" Is all she could muster up out of her mouth. Her fate was already decided. Now she just needed to know when she had to move.

"As soon as tomorrow. I gotta get out of here. Certain people know me around here and I can't chance anything happening out of my plans." There was silence when Ty said that. Jazmyn continued to stare at him and she noted the sad expression forming across his face. She immediately knew he was talking about Vanessa.

Oh, shit! Vanessa! As soon as Jazmyn thought her name, knocks sounded off at the door. Crimson and Dom jumped up; each of them had their hands on their weapons...ready to pull them out and bust a cap in the ass of whatever threat may have been standing there for them.

"No, it's ok! Let me handle this!" Jazmyn whispered to them. Once they settled down, she began walking over to answer the door, but it was too late. The handle swirled around and the door swung open. In walked Vanessa looking tired, but pretty much as flawless as she normally did.

"Jaz, I'm sorry I'm a little late, but why the hell you needed me to...." Her voice trailed off once she noticed that there were more people in the room behind Jazmyn. Jazmyn's heart dropped to the pit of her stomach when she saw Vanessa's eyes lock in on where she knew Ty was sitting. Vanessa's mouth dropped open and tears formed in her eyes immediately.

"Oh my God..." Vanessa was wavering and Jazmyn knew she was about to faint. She ran over to her just in time to catch her. Jazmyn held her for a minute silently. She was stunned and she didn't want to turn around.

"Jazmyn...what the fuck?!" Jazmyn squeezed her eyes closed and groaned inwardly at Dom's voice. She knew someone was sure to say something, but she wasn't ready to hear about this new major fuck up that she had caused. Jazmyn struggled as she tried to pull Vanessa up into her arms. The girl looked lightweight, but she was far from it.

Jazmyn turned when she felt someone tapping her on her shoulder. It was Ty.

"Let me hold her," he said. Jazmyn couldn't argue if she wanted to. He had tears in his eyes and the way he was looking at Vanessa was as if she was the only woman in the world. Jazmyn shifted her hands to allow him to hold her and he scooped Vanessa's body up with so much gentle strength and care that Jazmyn almost thought she would be emotional as well. Until she heard Dom's voice behind her.

"How the hell did this happen, Jay? Gotdamn!" Jazmyn turned around to look at him.

"I called her to come over before I knew you all were coming here. When you knocked, she was the one I was expecting! I wanted to ask her about how she didn't tell me she was working with you to have Dexter Malcolm killed." Jazmyn tried to explain but no matter what, it didn't seem to make a difference. Dom was obviously pissed. What surprised her though was that Crimson had a different expression on her face. She didn't seem upset at all. She didn't even seem focused on Jazmyn. Instead she was looking over at Ty as he held Vanessa. She had a look on her face that seemed to be a mixture of shock, hurt and disappointment. Any other time, Jazmyn would have been a little more intrigued by what was obviously a glimpse into what had to be a very entertaining backstory, but right now she was too interested in saving her own ass.

"Who the fuck is Dexter Malcolm? And why you didn't tell us she was coming after we got here?" Dom questioned. Jazmyn's face dropped. So they hadn't killed Dexter. Now she was confused and she felt dumb.

"Um...Well, I was a little surprised once I saw him." Jazmyn pointed over at Ty.

"When you saw him...wasn't that even more of a reason for you to open up your motherfuckin' mouth and...."

"Hey, it's all good." Ty said without looking away from Vanessa's face. "What's done is done. Now, let's get out of here." He stood up easily, still cradling Vanessa's body as if she were the most delicate and fragile thing on Earth. Dom stood up and followed behind him as they both headed to the door. Crimson stood up slowly and walked behind the two of them. She kept her head low and didn't say a word as she walked pass Jazmyn. Jazmyn lifted an eyebrow as she studied her.

Let me find out Crimson is in love with somebody! Jazmyn almost chuckled aloud at the thought. *Thought I would never see the day.* Jazmyn walked over to the door and slammed it behind them. This time she made sure to lock it so that she wouldn't have any other visitors barging in like they owned the place. She laid back against the door and thought to herself as she heard the engines of the car they arrived in crank up and drive off.

Fuck...I still have no idea who killed Dexter.

ALEXIS

"Oh….my…God!" Alexis gasped out loud as she looked at the television screen. She was in the middle of eating a wheat bagel with cream cheese when she saw the headline and started to tune in to the story. The headline read *Man Murdered at the Twelve hotel in Buckhead.* But that wasn't what alarmed her at all. She was alarmed by the fact that the picture that she was looking at was a photo of Dexter. An old one at that, but it was definitely him. The caption under the photo read: *Victim: Dexter Malcolm.* Alexis felt as if she was going to faint right in the middle of her kitchen as she looked at the small screen.

What's going on, baby?" Marc asked as he walked into the kitchen wearing nothing but pajama pants. He looked so different now than he had the night before. The night before he was all business. There was no "babys" or "darlings," everything and all things were serious. Today he was relaxed, cheerful, and happy. The mood shift was so drastic that Alexis wondered for a minute if he had multiple personalities.

Am I dating Dr. Jekyll and Mr. Hyde?

"I'm looking at the news. Dexter…he was killed last night." Alexis said slowly in a hushed voice. She was almost certain that Marc didn't hear her because he barely reacted.

"Really?" Marc asked as he pulled a carton of orange juice out of the refrigerator. He didn't bother getting a glass or anything; he just simply drunk it straight from the container. Alexis turned up her lips at him as she watched and tried to figure out when she started living in a frat house.

"Thirsty?"

"A little," He replied before twisting the cap back on and placing the carton back into the refrigerator.

"Well....aren't you a little surprised? About Dexter?" Alexis asked. She was beginning to grow suspicious of his actions. First, he had the top secret, ultra-suspect meeting last night with an old business partner and now, she had mentioned that Dexter had been murdered and he had nothing to say. Just the other day, Dexter was in their home and he and Marc were carrying on like the old friends they were. Now Dexter was dead and Marc was too busy leaning on the counter, reading over the morning's newspaper to care.

"Surprised? Not really. I don't care enough about him to be surprised. And after what you told me yesterday, I'm glad he's dead. I hope to hell he suffered." Alexis was shocked into silence. Marc had changed but she would have been lying if she said that she didn't like it a little.

"Marc, is everything okay with you? You seem...different," Alexis asked as she squinted at him. He was so sexy that she had completely forgotten her feelings about what she had seen on the news. She had wanted the bastard dead for what he did; she hadn't expected him to actually be dead though. She knew she should feel some type of way about that, but at the moment, all of her emotions were tied up into Marc.

"Listen, Lexi. I'm one way with you because you're my wife and I love you. I've always seen you as fragile and sheltered. You've always been that way. You haven't experienced shit...your little rich girl problems are just that: little ass rich girl problems. But the past few months have shown me something. What happened to you has made you think of me as less than a man because you don't think that I can protect you. Also, you've matured a lot and you've seen how the world can be. So, I can't treat you as fragile anymore because you're not." Marc shrugged as he finished his thought and looked back down at the paper.

"So you're saying I married a stranger? You've been pretending to be a certain way because of how you thought of me?" Alexis asked quietly.

"No, I'm saying you married a man who loves you. But yes, there is a lot of shit you don't know. And I keep that to myself on purpose to protect you." Marc said looking back up at her. Alexis stared back at him as she tried to digest what he was saying.

What secrets did he have? Was he having an affair? Was he on the down-low? What could it be?

"I need to know all of your secrets, Marc. I'm your wife. You have to tell me." Alexis begged.

"One day..." Marc said standing up straight. He grabbed the paper and placed it under his arm.

"When?" Alexis asked him.

"Lexi...you really should come with me on a business trip some-time." He said as he started to walk out of the kitchen.

Does he really want to discuss business now?

"Wait...Marc! I have to ask you something!" Alexis yelled just as Marc had rounded the corner to walk out of the kitchen.

"Yes?" He asked sticking his head back in.

"Did you kill Dexter? Or did you have him killed?" Alexis asked, looking deep into his eyes. She had to know.

"Baby, don't worry about all that...I'm sure that motherfucker didn't even know what was coming."

ALEXIS GROANED LOUDLY. THIS WAS THE SIXTH TIME IN A ROW THAT SHE had tried to call Vanessa and the phone continued to go directly to voicemail. She needed to speak to her sister about everything that was happening. Something was going on and she had to get to the bottom of it. Vanessa always knew what to do when shit hit the fan.

Alexis had just dropped her phone down on her bed when it rung again. Her spirits lifted immediately when she figured that it was her sister returning her call. Those hopes were dashed to hell when she saw the number glowing across the screen. She pressed the button to answer the call and placed the phone against her ear.

"What do you want?" Alexis said gruffly.

"My, my, Alexis...have you lost your manners? Well, I guess you don't really need any with your clientele." Alexis rolled her eyes as Ms. Juice's deep and raspy voice flowed through the speaker. She was about the last person on Earth that Alexis wanted to speak to right now.

Why did I answer the phone again?

"Well, since you answered, I'm guessing that somewhere in the mind of yours you are thinking you need to pay me a visit." Alexis rolled her eyes as she listened to the woman speak. However, she couldn't deny that part of it was true. She did need to blow off some steam. Between the last couple days, she had experienced so much stress that she could barely stand it all. She had tried to call Vanessa in order to speak to her about it, but it seemed as if Vanessa was doing her own thing and she was too busy to assist her only sister.

"Well, anyways...you have a few clients who have been asking about you and have threatened to stop perusing my establishment if you do not return. When are you planning on returning?" Alexis thought about the question for a while. Honestly, she didn't need to think all that hard. She wanted to get back. She needed to. She'd had too much going on and she felt like she would burst open if she didn't whoop somebody's ass ASAP.

"I'm on my way. " Alexis disconnected the call and then started to get up so that she could get ready to leave.

"You're on your way where?" Marc asked as he walked into the room. He stopped right in front of Alexis and looked down at her. Alexis felt like she had never realized until that moment how short she was in comparison to him. He frowned down at her as he waited for an answer.

"Out. I have something that I need to do." Alexis said as she rose up out of the bed and walked into the bathroom to take a shower. Marc didn't say anything else and she was grateful for that.

ALEXIS BEGAN TO GET EXCITED AS SOON AS SHE SAW THE ENTRANCE TO Ms. Juice's place. The large house was just the same as when she last left it: luxurious, bright, and full of the fantasies and sex-filled dreams of most of the high-paid residents in the Atlanta area. Alexis smiled once she swiped her key card that gave her access to the building.

"Well, look who it is!" Alexis looked up just in time to see Sharonda walking around the corner. She held her arms out and waited for Alexis to walk over and give her a hug. "I've miss you... damn, you can't call a bitch or anything, huh?"

"It's only been a few days, Sharonda...literally." Alexis said rolling her eyes with a laugh.

"Yes, but damn...you know days and nights here are long as hell!" Alexis nodded her head; she had to agree with her. Although Alexis was fortunate that she didn't need this place for money, so she could pretty much come and go as she pleased, she was well aware that many of the other women didn't have it like that so they spent most of their time in this house bouncing on dick after dick as they tried to make it to payday. That kind of stuff started to wear on you after a while. Sharonda was much younger than Alexis, but she looked at least the same age, if not older. And if you were to calculate up her experiences, she was definitely "older" than Alexis.

"We should go out or something after I'm done here...if you can take a break. I have a lot to catch you up on," Alexis said as she walked away from Sharonda and headed to her room to freshen up. "Can you tell Her Highness Juice that I'm here?" Alexis said with extreme sarcasm.

"I sure will. We will see about catching up later." Sharonda said behind her as she walked in the opposite direction towards the break area.

As soon as Alexis walked into her room, she felt the "head bitch" attitude kick in. She was ready to put a major ass kicking down on somebody and she was ready to get started. She stripped away her clothes quickly and walked over to the costume closet to pick out something special. The other girls had to share their lingerie, but Alexis spent good money making sure that she could secure her own outfits and that no one would be pulling her thongs up between their ass, but her.

While rubbing her lavender scented lotion on her body, she began to think about Marc and how much he'd changed. It was like night and day...the way he was in the past verses how he was now.

I guess he could say the same about me, she thought as she paused for a second to think about the drastic changes in her life that had occurred as a result of her rape. The thought made her think about Dexter. She had a good reason to suspect that her own husband had been the one responsible. Alexis pondered for a minute how she would feel if she knew for a fact that Marc was responsible for killing someone. She wasn't sure what to feel because she knew at that moment that if she had the opportunity, she probably would have put a bullet straight through Dexter's head also.

"Are you ready, Alexis?" Alexis heard Ms. Juice's voice over the intercom in her room. She placed the lotion bottle down beside her and walked over to the intercom to respond.

"I am. You can send the first one back," she responded before walking back over to put up the lotion bottle that she had been using. She took one final look at herself in the mirror before grabbing her whip and preparing herself for action. When Alexis heard knocking at the door, she tossed her hair over her shoulder and straightened her back.

"You may enter!" She said loudly and with the authority that she loved having by being in her position. The door batted open slowly and Alexis smiled once she saw the man enter. It was John, of course. But it was the John that she had seen at the restaurant the other day.

He had gotten severely out of line and Alexis was all too ready to teach him a lesson for trying to embarrass her in front of Vanessa, her husband, and a few other members of the general public.

"It's you...Well, you already know that you've been bad and I'm definitely going to make you pay. Take that shit off and get on the fucking bed!" Alexis shouted as she started walking over to the man. He frowned at her and that only pissed her off even more. In this room, she was in charge. He was never to oppose her; he was only to obey without question. She took one look over at him. He was dressed in another power suit, his blond hair was tousled over his head, and his green eyes bore deep into her. His lips curled up into a sneer as he continued to look.

"Did you not hear what the fuck I told you? I said *take that shit off and get on the bed!*" Alexis repeated. She reached back and backhanded him as hard as he could right across the face. She was barely able to brace herself before he grabbed her by her neck and pulled her close to him.

"You think I came here for that shit bitch? I'm done with your ass. I've been done since I saw how weak and stupid you looked at the restaurant the other day...hiding behind your lame ass husband and that other bitch! I came here to finally get my money's worth from you!" With that, the man pushed Alexis backwards hard onto the bed and quickly ran forward. He placed his body on top of her and pinned her down by holding both of her tiny wrists into one of his massive hands. He used the other hand to tear at the black leather thong that she was wearing.

Alexis wanted to scream out but she couldn't. Tears welled up in her eyes as she felt the man pulling at his own pants to release his dick that was hard and ready to violate her.

This can't be happening to me. Not again. This can't be happening. Alexis tried to focus on other things in the room. She tried to relax her body in hopes that whatever this man meant to do would end quickly if she didn't resist. But then the panic kicked in.

Alexis started writhing and fighting back. She opened her mouth and prepared to let out a loud scream but it was cut short as he grabbed her tightly by her throat. But still she fought. She kicked and squirmed as much as she could. She was determined that this could not happen to her again.

"Alexis!" Alexis stopped for a minute when she heard her name. She recognized the voice. But it couldn't be who she thought it was, so she knew that John must have had such a grip on her throat that the lack of oxygen must have been making her imagine things.

Suddenly John was lifted off of her from behind. For a brief moment, he kept his grip on her neck, which lifted her in the air a little, but once surprise and shock kicked in for John, he quickly released her. Alexis fell back on the bed and wasted no time scurrying over to the edge, as far away as she could from John. After taking a few quick breaths, she was able to focus her eyes on what was going on. A man was pounding his fists over and over again into John. Alexis gasped out loud.

"Marc?" Alexis stared as her husband laid punch after punch into John, who appeared to either be unconscious or faking death in order to escape the severe beat-down he was getting. Marc seemed to have been in a trance, he didn't look as if he had any awareness of anything around him other than the man that he was pounding with his fist. Alexis knew she had to do something or Marc would kill him.

"Marc! Stop!" She yelled loudly. At that moment, Marc stopped just short of landing another punch on the man's already swollen and bruised face. He looked up at Alexis and she grimaced once she saw the anger and hate behind his eyes. She almost didn't recognize him until his eyes softened as he realized he was looking at his wife.

"Baby...are you ok?" He said slowly as he walked over to her. Alexis remained in her position and did not move. She knew that her husband would never harm her, but in the past two days, he was full of so many surprises that she was unsure how to react with him. Alexis' eyes darted over to the man that was lying on the floor. Other than the swelling and the purple and red bruises on his light skin, he seemed to be sleeping peacefully otherwise. She saw him reach down and grab something before he pulled away from the man.

"Marc, what are you doing?" Marc noticed the look of disgust on her face as she stared at the man lying unconscious behind him.

"I had to...Lexi. He was about to hurt you." He said. He reached out his hand to her. Alexis eyes him suspiciously before reaching out her own hand in response. Before he could grab it the door swung open. Ms. Juice entered holding something that appeared to be a small pistol in the air. She pointed it at Marc before looking around the room. Once she saw John's body, her mouth fell open.

"What the fuck?! Is he...dead?" She asked walking forward; her pistol was still aimed directly at Marc's face, but he didn't flinch at all. Alexis stared at Marc incredulously.

This guy doesn't have his hands in the air or anything. He looks pretty comfortable for a man with a damn gun shoved in his face!

"He's not dead. When I walked in here, he was trying to rape my wife." Marc said gesturing over at Alexis.

"Your *wife?*" Ms. Juice asked. She looked over at Alexis for a response. Alexis nodded her head to confirm that Marc was her husband. Ms. Juice exhaled loudly and lowered her gun. "Damn! He was one of my best customers," she said as she looked at the John on the floor. The man started snoring loudly and Ms. Juice sucked her teeth. "We will just leave his ass right here until he comes to. I got something for him. He is about to pay me out of the ass for trying to rape one of my girls."

"About that....Alexis will no longer be "one of your girls." Baby, let's go." Marc beckoned over to Alexis and she got up from the corner of the bed and walked over to him. He pulled a long coat from off the top of the long cherry wood dresser near the door and draped it around her.

"Yeah, whatever. This motherfucker still gone pay me my..." Ms. Juice continued as they walked out of the door. Alexis looked up at Marc as they walked out of the building and to his car.

"I will have someone pick up your car later," he mumbled to her as he opened the door for her to get into the passenger side. She had a lot of questions, but she wasn't sure it was the time to ask. She decided to wait until later.

KAYLEN

*K*aylen tried to compose herself but it was proving rather difficult since she was sure that her jaw was dragging on the floor. To say she was shock would be an understatement. To say that she was embarrassed would be saying the absolute least. To say that she was pissed would be the most ridiculous way that anyone could ever describe her current situation. Her emotions were not that simple. On a scale of 1 to 100, shocked was a 5, embarrassed was a 2, pissed was a 10, but she was a 100.

This bitch done fucked with the wrong one! Kaylen thought to herself as she looked at the video that Caleb was playing her for the second time. In all honesty, she didn't need to see it, she had lived it. But she was perplexed by the fact that he had such a video in his possession that she just had to see it again. She squinted her eyes as she tried to digest everything that had just happened within the last few hours.

Kaylen had woke up abnormally early that morning. Something just didn't feel right and she couldn't continue to sleep. When she rose out of the bed and saw that even Tiny couldn't elevate her mood, she knew that she was going to be in for an extra bit of bullshit today. Less than an hour later, her phone rang. She answered it, knowing full well who it was before pressing "answer."

"Yes, Caleb?" she said drily. She was still feeling a little salty about the fact that after he and Tiffany hashed out their issues in front of her townhome; he had left with her stating that he needed to see his daughter and they had things to discuss. Granted, Kaylen understood him needing to see his daughter, but her question was, did the bitch mother always have to be lurking around as well? Apparently, that was Tiffany's preference and Caleb was too afraid to demand anything different.

"I'm coming over."

"Well, I just woke up, so….." Kaylen stopped when she realized that the line had gone dead. Confused, she pulled the phone away from her ear and looked at it as if it would give her answers.

I know this nigga didn't just hang up on me! She thought as she placed the phone on the counter. But he had definitely hung up on her and the next time she saw Caleb, he was standing in front of her holding up his cellphone in front of her face. On the screen was a video of her and Zo having sex. It was a fairly bad view, since the person who recorded it had been standing outside. Unfortunately, Kaylen's blinds weren't pulled tight enough to avoid catching a decent angle with the cellphone that was used to record the action. It hadn't taken Kaylen long at all to figure out who had decided to play paparazzi.

"That *bitch* recorded me? The hell? You need to learn how to control your ghetto ass babymama!" Kaylen said grabbing the phone out of Caleb's hands so that she could take a closer look.

"That's what the fuck you're focused on, Kay?" Caleb yelled. The sound of his voice jarred Kaylen's attention. He sounded close to tears. She had never heard him sound that way. She'd never really seen him get this emotional. Sure, she had seen him when he was happy…even when he was down, but she had never seen him hurt or near tears. And especially not about a woman.

"Oh, Caleb….I'm sorry." She didn't know what to say beyond that. The truth was that she was upset that she hurt him, but it needed to be done. She didn't love him the way that he needed and she did not want to get married. She hadn't even had the chance to be in a relationship with Zo, but she was already certain that she had greater feelings for him than she currently did for Caleb.

"That's it? You're sorry?" Caleb asked. He had tears in his eyes. "All that shit you gave me about other women when I was away at the conference. I had to put up with that when I knew I wasn't doing anything. I didn't even have the urge. I didn't want to get into a relationship for this reason. You can't trust women! I knew that shit, but I thought you were worth it. Now look at this shit...you fucked another nigga and the best you can say to me is that you're sorry?" Kaylen wanted to cry, but the tears wouldn't come. In that moment, she was more relieved than anything that this was happening. She hated for Caleb to be in pain, but this had to happen and she couldn't stop it.

"And where the fuck is your ring?!" Caleb yelled as he looked at her hand. Kaylen's heart jumped to her throat.

Shit! I forgot I took it off!

"It's...uh...it's in the car." Kaylen mumbled. She looked down to the ground at her feet. She couldn't bear to look at Caleb in that moment. She knew that it would break her heart to see him hurt like he was hurting. She had been hurt by him all those years when she wanted him so bad, but he wouldn't commit. The difference is that he never lied to her about it. The hurt was brought on by herself as much as him because she knew the deal and stayed. In this instance, it was all her fault. She had lied to him and pretended that she felt ways that she did not.

"Kay?" Caleb said her name in a way that demanded her attention. It almost seemed as if he was pleading and no matter what, Kaylen felt the need to look up at him. Once she did, she nearly crumbled under the gravity of emotion that was coming from his eyes. One lone tear had rolled down his face and was hovering over his mouth. Kaylen felt her eyes tear up and she exhaled loudly as she tried not to buckle under the burden of guilt that she felt. "I just want you to know that I loved you. I really did." And with that, Caleb turned around and walked out of her living room, out of her townhome and out of her life.

JAZMYN

*J*azmyn rubbed her eyes as she tried to allow them to adjust to the light. It had only been a few hours since Crimson and Dom had left with Ty and Vanessa. She had tried to get some sleep, but unfortunately it was now being interrupted by the shrill ring of her phone. She groaned loudly before rolling over to grab her cellphone off of her nightstand.

"Hello?" Jazmyn grumbled into the phone. She frowned her face and smacked her lips at how dry her mouth felt. She had a metallic taste in her mouth and she knew from that point that somebody was calling with the bullshit. Whenever a shit-storm was coming her way, her body had a way of warning her beforehand.

"I need you to get here now! They are taking her...they are taking my baby away from me!" Jazmyn sat straight up in her bed as she tried to digest what he was saying. Her mind shifted to attorney mode immediately. Something didn't make sense about this.

"Wait, Kingston, calm down! They can't take her from you...we didn't go to court or anything. A judge would have to rule on it in order for her to be taken fro..."

"Fuck that Jaz! Listen to me...there is a white lady standing in my

142

fucking house right now packing up my daughter's shit. She is saying that she is taking her from me and she has some judge's signed paperwork in her hand. She even has a police officer with her. I know you're a lawyer! I'm a fucking lawyer too! But that shit doesn't matter. They are taking her away from me right now!" Kingston yelled into the phone. Jazmyn could tell by his voice that he was crying. She had no idea what to do and she knew that if he saw her looking like she was at that exact moment; hair every which way on top of her head, drool still stuck to the side of her face, pillowcase patterns imprinted on her forehead and her mouth hanging wide open, he would probably have wanted to slap the shit out her for being so worthless.

"I will be there in 15 minutes." Jazmyn said immediately into the phone. She waited on the line for Kingston to say something, but he just hung up the call. She jumped out of bed and started trying to do a rush job of getting herself together.

There probably isn't much I can do, but at least I can be present to pick Kingston 's ass up off the floor after they walk outta there with LaShea.

JAZMYN SHIFTED UNCOMFORTABLY IN HER SEAT. SHE HAD NO IDEA WHAT to do or say. She was not good when it came to dealing with people's emotions. Most times she even tried to suppress her own emotions because she had no idea how to deal with her own. Her usual response when someone got emotional was to either leave the room or find out who she had to kill. Unfortunately, she didn't think that either option was available in this situation.

She took another worried glance over at Kingston. He was sitting in his favorite leather recliner; he loved it because he said it was the most comfortable thing that he had ever sat in. But today, he looked anything but relaxed. His green eyes were rimmed with red and he had a blank stare on his face that chilled Jazmyn to the bone. It looked like his soul was gone. He looked like he was nothing but a shell of a person. One who had been hurt to the core and didn't see any way to possibly move on. Jazmyn knew there was something that she needed to do, but she had no idea what.

Kaylen would know. Hell, the old Alexis would even know. Shit....I wonder if I can give them a call. Jazmyn reached down to her purse to grab her phone, but was interrupted when the doorbell rang.

Not again...please. Jazmyn glanced over at Kingston before getting up to answer the door. Although he had adjusted in his seat and seemed to have been a tad more alert than he was seconds ago, he hadn't bothered making any movements related to checking on who was outside the door.

Jazmyn looked out the peephole and saw an UPS delivery man standing outside. She said a silent prayer that he was coming with good news; she wasn't greedy though, even news that was neither good nor bad would have been fine at the moment. But she knew for a fact that Kingston could not take any more bad news.

"Yes, why are you here?" Jazmyn said once the door was open. There was no time for small talk or being friendly. She had a situation on her hands and was ready to call her friends to figure out a way to handle it.

"Package for Kingston Grey." The man said as he rudely shoved the pad in her face to have her sign for the package. Jazmyn frowned at him before taking the stylus and quickly signing her name. She thrust it back at him and he handed her a medium-sized boxed.

"Spell your last name for me."

"T-A-Y-L-O-R," Jazmyn replied quickly before slamming the door in his face. Once she locked the door behind her, she turned to look at Kingston. He seemed to be trying to gather himself together and Jazmyn felt a small sense of relief.

"Baby, do you want something to eat or something? Drink?" Jazmyn asked as she cocked her head to the side and waited for his reply. He jumped as if he didn't know she was standing there, then sighed heavily and rubbed his nose with the sleeve of his shirt.

"No. What is that?" Kingston asked her. He didn't look at her, but she assumed that he was referring to the UPS package in her hands.

"I don't know. Here…it's something for you." Jazmyn walked over to him and handed him the box. "I will go get you some scissors." She said as she walked into the kitchen.

"No need." Kingston said as he started to rip open the box. Jazmyn shrugged and walked to the kitchen to find something to eat. She opened the refrigerator to see if there was anything easy that she could make. Cooking was definitely not her strongpoint, but she knew she could make some eggs or something. Maybe a slice of buttered toast would suffice. Jazmyn pulled out the butter, eggs, milk, and orange juice before surveying the refrigerator one last time to see if there were any other ingredients available to make the miracle of her making a meal happen.

"Are you sure you don't want anything?" Jazmyn asked Kingston. She heard movement behind her so she figured that he was up and moving and may have been in the mood for a meal.

"Jazmyn! What the fuck is this?!" Kingston roared from behind her. Jazmyn stopped in her tracks. She picked her head up and looked straight ahead in shock. She was too afraid to turn around to see what he was referring to because she knew that only a few things regarding her would make him upset enough to yell at her in that way.

"Jazmyn! I'm fucking talking to you!" The next thing Jazmyn knew, Kingston had grabbed her by the upper arm and flipped her around so fast that she knocked the carton of eggs to the floor. They fell to the tile floor so hard that it was a certainty that every egg in the carton was most likely broken. The carton of milk that Jazmyn had been holding fell to the floor on her foot and the liquid began pouring out over her toes, but it didn't matter because her eyes were focused on what Kingston was waving in front of her. Tears came to her eyes immediately and she was too dazed and confused to even think about stopping them. She felt her heart beating so hard that it was certain to beat out of her chest at some point. The icy feeling on her back crept all the way up to the top of head and she began to feel cold as the realization of what was happening set upon her.

Kingston was holding a collage of photos in his hand. Some of the pictures were the photos from over ten years ago when she had killed a politician. They were the same photos that she had killed Shanice for sending to her home. Or she thought it had been Shanice that sent them. She figured Shanice was blackmailing her and she settled the situation by following Crimson and Dom's orders to kill her because she posed a threat to all of them. Jazmyn hadn't thought there was anyone else who would want to blackmail her at that point but Shanice since Jazmyn was sleeping with her husband and had also dragged her ass out of her vehicle and beat her down in front of a couple dozen people.

The other photos were the ones that chilled Jazmyn to the bone. She wasn't sure if Kingston fully understood what the pictures meant, but if he had found out for some reason, Jazmyn knew that she would be in a huge unexplainable predicament. There were about five photos of her sneaking up to Kingston's home and creeping into what had eventually become LaShea's bedroom. There were photos of the day that LaShea was born and Shanice was murdered at her hands. They showed vivid images of Jazmyn creeping into the home and also when she left the house, walked over to her vehicle, and drove away.

He can't know from these photos that I killed her, right? Jazmyn thought to herself. She was trying to pull at any hope that she could to reassure her that this situation wasn't as bad as she thought it was. The last shred of hope was dashed to shit when she saw that each photo was time and date stamped. Kingston was an attorney and a damn good one. He had an eye for detail. He could put two and two together to see that Jazmyn had killed in the past, and it was nothing for her to kill again. She was in the home during the time when Shanice was killed and she had been the only one there. The tears started overflowing from out of her eyes with such force that Jazmyn couldn't see anything at all. Her whole body buckled and she fell to the floor. She had trouble breathing and she started heaving forcefully as she tried to grasp at any air that she could to fill her lungs. She felt like she was dying and Kingston didn't even move to help her.

"So it's true! You sneaky, crazy, fucked up little bitch! This letter explained it all. You killed some guy when you were *sixteen years old?*

What are you...some kinda of psycho killer? And Shanice...." Kingston paused and Jazmyn could hear him start weeping. She tried her hardest to steady her breathing and get herself together, but she couldn't. It felt like she was having a panic attack. There was so much pressure on her head that she couldn't lift it, so she just laid down on the ground.

"You killed Shanice for no reason but that you're a crazy ass psycho bitch! Get the fuck out of here. I'm handing all of this evidence over to the cops and I hope to God they lock your ass up for the rest of your life. I *can't believe* that you came in here and raised Shanice's baby when all the time, you knew you killed her mother in this very house....in the same room that we sleep in. You are fucked up and I can't believe this...get the fuck out!" Kingston roared and Jazmyn felt him grab her around her neck. He started dragging her through the kitchen and towards the front door like a sack of garbage. The burn of the carpet rubbing against her skin made her struggle against his grasp and she tried to stand up. He had a firm grip on the back of her neck, but she had to try to say something. It was a struggle, but she needed Kingston to listen to her.

"Kingston, stop! Please...you don't understand. I didn't want to do it...I had to! Baby, please believe me, I was just trying to protect us!" Jazmyn's pleas fell on deaf ears because Kingston continued pulling her through the living room. He paused only for a second to grab her purse and her keys before continuing to drag her to the door.

"I will be changing the locks, Jazmyn. Don't try to come back here or I will shoot your crazy ass myself."

"Baby, you have to let me explain! It's not what you think, baby. It's not..." Jazmyn's screams were cut short when Kingston opened the door and slung her outside as if she weighed nothing at all. He dropped her purse and keys next to her and then shut the door. Jazmyn sat there for a moment trying to adjust to what had just occurred. She heard the door swing open again and a sliver of hope flickered in her heart. It was gone just as quickly when she saw Kingston throw her black Michael Kors' heels outside next to her before slamming the door shut again and locking it. Jazmyn couldn't pull herself together enough to move. She couldn't wrap her mind around what had just happened. She had never thought this day would come and she couldn't bear to deal with it. So she simply lay down on the concrete where Kingston had left her and continued to weep.

ALEXIS

"We need to talk." Alexis looked up at Marc as he stood above her. She had been spending her day lying in bed feeling sorry for herself and confused about her husband. As soon as they had gotten back home, she headed straight up to the bedroom and closed the door. She didn't know what to say to Marc. She knew there was a change in him and that he had secrets, but she wasn't sure how to approach the subject with him again or whether he would be willing to share anything this time. At the same time, she wasn't sure if she really wanted to know whether or not he had killed Dexter.

"What do we need to talk about?" Alexis asked as she sat up on the bed. She was apprehensive about the discussion and had no idea what to expect or what her reaction would be when she found out, but she knew that if Marc was ready to speak, she needed to hear it now rather than later.

"Ok." Marc sighed heavily and then sat down at the foot of the bed. He paused for a long time as if he were trying to think about what he wanted to say. Alexis waited in anticipation.

"Lexi, there is a lot that I need to tell you about my life. I..uh…well, I should have told you this a long time ago. So I can understand if you want to leave me after I do. I feel like we are in a place where we are trying to repair our marriage. We are trying to reveal our secrets and move on...together, hopefully." Alexis sat up straighter in the bed. She was confused. What exactly did he want to tell her that could make her want to leave him? He had just found out that she had been working in a brothel...and now he was talking about her leaving him for something he had done...the hell? She figured it could only be one thing.

"You murdered Dexter, didn't you?" Alexis asked. She felt like that was the only thing that he could admit to that he would think she would leave him for. He was wrong...she was shocked because she would have never thought that Marc had it in him. But for some reason, though Dexter had been her friend, she couldn't bring herself to mourn her rapists' death.

"Let me explain this first, Alexis. There is a lot that you don't know about me. I need to tell you." Marc adjusted nervously on the bed before beginning again. "My family business...I've never told you about what it is that we do. I've never really spoke to you about my job."

"You are the Vice President of Sales...for your parent's company. I already know that." Alexis responded. She was genuinely confused at this point. She didn't understand why they were talking about what he did for a living. She already knew.

"No, well...not exactly. The reason that I've never spoke about the details on what I do at work is that it is not as innocent as a simple job. My family is a part of an illegal operation. Extortion, grand theft auto, drug trafficking. You name it....we are involved. That's how we make our money. I'm in charge of overseeing our sales operations. Which means that I make sure that we have some heavy hitters on our side...government officials, celebrities, people of status or who have influence so that they can help run our operations. I also make sure that everything is going right on the financial side. I've been wanting to share this with you for a while. I always ask you to go with me when I leave for business...I've been trying to figure out how to tell you." Marc paused and Alexis struggled to try to figure out exactly it was that he was telling her.

"So, what are you trying to say? Are you saying that your family is a part of the mafia or mob or something? I don't get it. What is going on?" Alexis asked.

"Yes. That's exactly what I'm trying to tell you. Well...we don't really refer to ourselves as the mob or the mafia, but we do a lot of the same things. We are just...the Sorianos. And we establish power and control by all means necessary. It's organized crime, but everyone that has power or money in this country partakes in organized crime. No one is absolutely innocent and able to make it in this world." He became quiet and Alexis did not rush in to fill in the silence. She had a lot on her mind. Although she had heard a lot about the mafia, she didn't know too much about being a part of a "mafia family" entailed. Her life hadn't seemed like she was a part of a crime family. Then again, she didn't accompany Marc on business trips and she rarely saw her in-laws, so it made sense that she would have no idea.

"Well, this had never affected me so....I don't really know how to react to it. I mean, I guess as long as the Atlanta PD don't come in busting through our doors, I'm fine." Alexis shrugged. Marc tossed his head back and let out a loud thunderous laugh. Alexis blinked a few times as she struggled to figure out what was so funny.

"Lexi, this is far bigger than the Atlanta PD so I know you definitely do not understand. Our operations are way bigger than them; it's bigger than the Feds. If any force is going to try to take us down, it's going to be the...I don't know...the fucking army or something." Marc continued to laugh and Alexis' eyes grew big with surprise. "And that wouldn't even happen, baby, because we have government officials on our team. Don't worry, we got this." Alexis continued to stare at him. He cleared his throat and then became serious again.

"But here is the thing. We have to move." Alexis blinked at him a few times and then frowned deeply.

"What, Marc? What the hell are you saying?" Alexis kicked the covers off of her legs and prepared to stand up. He was saying too much at one time and she was unable to process everything correctly. "Why do we have to move?"

"This is why." Marc said as he held something up in his hand.

Alexis stared at it. It was a driver's license of some man. She looked closer. It was John. The man that tried to rape her. The same man that Marc had severely beaten back at Ms. Juice's place.

"Yeah, ok. Well, why do we have to move?" Alexis asked as she stood over him with her hand on her hip.

"I took his wallet out of his pocket before we left. It was my intention to send someone to finish him for trying to rape you. When I called my guy, he told me that this man is a Pachelli. I didn't put two and two together because apparently he uses his mother's last name." Marc paused and Alexis continued to give him a confused look.

Who are the Pachellis? Did I go to sleep and wake up in some Italian mobster movie? What the fuck just happened?

"The Pachellis are technically related to us. My mother's maiden name is Pachelli. Her father was one of the biggest mobsters in New York until around the 60s. During the 60s, my father's family, the Sorianos, started establishing power. My grandfather on my dad's side was smarter and he made relationships with key people extremely fast. Both of my grandfather's hated each other and it was war between then. Somewhere down the line, my mother and father met and started secretly dating. When my mother became pregnant with me, they ran away and eloped. Her father never recovered from losing his only daughter and my grandfather on my dad's side was able to establish ultimate control that way. Once my father took over, our reach expanded to enormous lengths and now we are worldwide. We are involved in things that I probably will never be able to tell you about. Not because I can't, but because I don't want you to know." Marc grew quiet as he seemed to reflect on those things.

"Anyways, this man...the one from Ms. Juice's home. He is a Pachelli. And he has the resources to find us. We need to move. I have to keep you safe." By the time that Marc stopped speaking, Alexis' mouth was hanging wide open. She felt like she was in a dream...just a few weeks ago, her life was normal compared to what she was learning now. She wanted to jump in the bed, pull the covers over her head, and go back to the normal life. Unfortunately, she was sure that she wouldn't ever be able to return to that at this point.

"I just need to sit down for a minute." Alexis said as she put her hand up to her forehead. She felt hot even though it was average temperature in the house. She could feel beads of sweat popping up at her hairline. Her stomach started turning and she had a funny taste in her mouth. Marc was staring at her with a face of absolute concern and guilt. She started to move closer to him so that he could hold her. At that moment, she needed to feel something familiar and something that had a "normal" feel to it.

Suddenly, Marc's expression changed to one of alarm and fear. Alexis stopped in her tracks when she saw the change and her eyebrows furrowed indicating her confusion.

"Alexis!!! GET THE FUCK DOWN, NOW!" Marc yelled.

"Huh?" She said as she looked down at her body. It was just about covered with red dots. Her eyes widened as she realized the gravity of the situation. Before she could react, Marc jumped up from the bed and tackled her to the floor. Alexis grunted loudly as she fell, but she was still able to hear the loud noise of a bullets shattering through her bedroom windows before implanting themselves in the wall right behind where she had been.

"Get the fuck in the closet, right now! Crawl to it. Do not move until I come get you out. Go, now!" Marc yelled. Alexis hesitated for a second. She was stunned and shocked.

Were those fucking bullets that just came through my house? Her brain couldn't correctly understand the severity of what was occurring. It seemed absolutely ridiculous and she thought that maybe she had imagined it until she looked over and saw all the shattered glass.

"Alexis! Move your ass...NOW!" Marc yelled again to her. Alexis rolled over to her stomach and started doing an army crawl to the closet. Once she made it in, she looked out just in time to see Marc grabbing all types of guns from hidden places in their bedroom. She had lived in this home for over five years and had no idea that there were so many secret crevices holding so many weapons of mass destruction.

What the hell is going on? What the fuck have I gotten myself into? She thought as she watched her husband run out of the room.

KAYLEN

"So...are you sure that you're ok?" Zo asked as he watched Kaylen in the kitchen. She was mixing up a drink that she had learned how to make from Jazmyn. Jazmyn called it the "Dick Rider"; named for the fact that it had a good dose of Tequila which always made her horny as hell.

"I'm great. Why do you keep asking me that?" Kaylen said looking back in Zo's direction. He was staring back at her as if she was mentally ill.

"Well, your fiancé saw a recorded video of us having sex and he broke off the engagement with you. You called me after and you sounded distressed. Now I'm here and you are in a cheerful mood in the kitchen making Bahama Mamas...which by the way, doesn't sound like shit I would ever drink." Zo said sitting back in his seat. Kaylen tried to stifle her laugh.

Wonder what you would think if you knew the actual name for this drink was "Dick Rider." She grinned to herself.

"Well...You don't think that's a little strange?" He asked.

"No, actually. I've been trying to tell you that I didn't want to marry Caleb. I felt like I was rushed into it. After everything that happened with Salem...he was there. He was the one that I had to carry me through it all." Kaylen looked at Zo and saw him drop his head. She knew that he probably felt guilty for not being there for her, but it was the truth. Caleb was around to pick up the pieces of her that were damaged after Salem had died and she was grateful for that.

"I'm sorry about that, Kay. I really do regret that I wasn't in the right headspace to help you when all that shit went down after Salem...died." Zo paused for a minute and Kaylen continued mixing the drinks.

"I do want to let you know that I came for you. After I heard you were being released from jail, I was there to pick you up, but I saw Caleb was there for you. So....I just left." Kaylen's head jerked up when she heard that.

I knew it! I felt that I was being watched and I KNEW it was Zo! Whenever Zo was around, it was like she could sense his presence. She felt him near her and it was amazing. The night she was released, she had that feeling. But she didn't see him so she forgot about it. Now she knew.

"Well, you could have called." Kaylen responded. Although she didn't harbor any ill feelings towards him, part of her still felt a little salty about the fact that Zo hadn't bothered to text her or even call to check up on her at all since the night he killed Salem. She knew he had a lot going on and had to deal with that fact that he had murdered his best friend. But he had to know that she was dealing with some heavy shit as well. They could have helped each other get through it. Instead he distanced himself from her.

"You're right. I could have called. That is my fault. But I do want to say this to you..."

"Hold on a minute. I'm coming." Kaylen grabbed the glasses and walked over to Zo. She handed him his drink and then sat down across from him. She pulled her legs up and laid them on the ottoman as she sipped the drink. The taste was even better than she had remembered. "Ok, I'm ready," she smiled.

"I thought about you every single day. I've been keeping up with you whether you believe it or not. I'm not on some stalker-type shit, but I do ask your friends about you just to make sure that you're safe.

I've asked them not to tell you that I check in on you and I'm grateful that they respect my wishes. Anyways, I feel strongly about you and I think that we should see if this thing can work. It never was just about sex to me. But anyways, I'm going to give you some time...to deal with this Caleb shit because I know that can't be over just like that for you. Then when you are ready, I'm here." Zo finished what he was saying and took a sip of his drink.

"Damn, this shit is pretty good," he said with a small chuckle before taking another sip.

"Yeah, I told you so!" Kaylen laughed and leaned back in her chair. As soon as she got comfortable her doorbell rang.

"Dammit!" She exclaimed. The sound of the doorbell surprised her and made her spill some of her drink on her lap.

"You want me to get it?" Zo asked her. Kaylen shook her head. The last thing she needed was for Caleb to be at the door and him and Zo get into it right in the front lawn.

"No, I got it. I'll be right back." Kaylen leaned over and placed her drink on a coaster atop her coffee table and the jotted over to the front door. She tried to look through the peephole, but whoever was at the door had their hand over it.

This better not be Tiffany's hoe ass playing at my door again. I'm about to beat this bitches ass up and down Atlanta! Kaylen hurriedly unlocked the door and swung it open with force as she prepared to kick some ass.

But it was not Tiffany at the door.

The person who was at the door was someone that Kaylen had never expected to see again a day in her life. Her mouth fell open and she blinked hard as she tried to ensure that her eyes were not playing tricks on her. She felt like she was having a bad case of deja-vu and she prayed to God that soon it would be over. Kaylen felt a sharp pain in her chest and she pressed her hand against it as she winced in pain.

"Oh my God! Oh..my God. Nooooo!" Kaylen gasped as she tried to deal with the fear that was crippling her.

I have to be seeing things. This can't be. Am I imagining this? Did I have that much to drink?

156

"Kaylen? Baby, what's wrong?" Kaylen heard Zo getting up from his seat and running over to where she stood. She wanted to tell him not to come but she couldn't make her brain cooperate with her mouth so she stayed silent.

"Oh my fucking, go....Salem?!" Zo said as he stopped behind her. "What the fuck?" Kaylen looked up in utter shock. Standing right in front of her face was Salem, looking fine as ever, not at all like the cracked out addict that he was the last time she had seen him. He looked amazing, angry, betrayed, but most importantly, he looked anything but dead. He looked back at the both of them with a deep frown on his face as he assessed the situation in front of him. Then his lips curved into a smile.

"Zo, so I guess you been doing pretty well, my nigga! This bitch right here got some good pussy, don't she?"

JAZMYN

*A*fter allowing her to lie on his front porch for over two hours, Kingston had finally had the decency to stuff her into her car and drive her home. He'd carried her into her home and dropped her on the sofa in her living room before turning around and leaving. Jazmyn had laid in that same spot for hours lamenting over her life. She couldn't move, it was like she was paralyzed in space being weighed down by all of her sins.

I killed the wrong one. I killed the wrong one. I killed the wrong one. The thought kept circling around in her head. She'd killed many people, but they all had it coming. They had all lived a life, causing absolute devastation to others by either assisting them with getting strung out on drugs, robbing and killing each other or by making political and business moves that allowed for these same things to happen. But that was not the case with Shanice. Jazmyn had killed someone who hadn't done any of these things...her worst crime that Jazmyn knew of was the fact that she had slept around on her husband. Hardly shit worth dying for.

Jazmyn had been able to reconcile killing her in her mind when she thought it was being done to save herself. She had tried to reason with herself that Shanice had done something that she shouldn't have and Crimson wouldn't stop until she was dead; so there was no need to feel bad about it. But the reality of it is that Jazmyn had *told* Crimson that Shanice was involved and that was the reason why she had to kill her. She had made that assumption with absolutely no evidence.

"Oh, my God…please forgive me. Please, please…please!" Jazmyn cried. She felt so alone and the guilt was eating at her. Every bad thing that was weighing on her seemed to be hovering above her head. She had never felt bad about anything that she had ever done. But now, it seemed as if all of the guilt that she should have felt, all the anxiety, every bit of it was pulling at her now. She pulled herself up from the sofa and walked over to her bar. She had a large bottle of Crown Royal left in the cabinet so she decided that it would be best to poor herself some shots and fall asleep.

Everything will be better in the morning.

Two hours later, the bottle was empty and Jazmyn still was not sleeping. Instead she was holding her phone and sobbing because Kingston had sent her straight to voicemail once again. She had been calling him every couple minutes for the past hour and he had not picked up once. She couldn't bear to listen to his voice on the voice-mail service long enough to actually leave a message, so she just hung each time and called right back.

"Please, Kingston. I need you…please pick up. Please!" She pleaded in the silent and dark room. She had pulled off all of her clothing and was lying in her panties and bra, spread across her bed as if the two ends of her body were being pulled in different directions. She was in total despair and the one person who could pull her out of it wasn't answering her calls.

Nobody loves me.

Jazmyn rolled around again and flicked through the contact list on her phone. A feeling was creeping up on her and she knew that it was nothing good. She knew that she needed to speak to someone at that exact moment or shit would not end well. She needed someone who loved her to pull her out of this dark place. She pressed the button to call Alexis. The phone rang and rang. Jazmyn's heart dropped to the pit of her stomach.

"You've reached Alexis. Sorry that I can't come to the pho...." Jazmyn ended the call.

"Nooo....please, Lexi. Please pick-up!" she tried dialing again. This time the call went directly to voicemail. Jazmyn closed her eyes and banged her fist against her forehead. She needed help and she needed it quickly. Her mind was thinking things that she knew were wrong, but she was unable to push the thoughts away. She dialed Kaylen's number and prayed that she would answer.

"Uh...Jazzy, I gotta call you back later. Bye!" Kaylen said in a rushed whisper.

"No, Kaylen! No, I need you. I need you to help me! Wait....please!" Jazmyn yelled into the phone. Her pleas fell on death ears. The line was dead. Jazmyn threw the phone down on the bed and covered her face with her hands. She started crying so hard that her body was moving like she was convulsing. She felt like she was going to throw up. She sniffed and rubbed at her eyes with the back of her hand before grabbing the phone again. This time she dialed someone that she could always depend on.

"Mama, please pick-up the phone. Please, please, please!" Jazmyn cried as she heard the ringing. The phone continued to ring and Jazmyn cried harder and harder. "Nooo, I need you! Please, God, help me! Please make her pick up the phone! Please!"

"Hi, you've reached my phone, but I ain't here..." Jazmyn ended the call and continued to wail loudly in the room.

Nobody loves me. Nobody loves me.

Wait....

There was one last person that she wanted to call. Jazmyn prayed that he would be the one to help her. He had helped once before in her life and she thought that maybe...just maybe, he could do it again. She scrolled through her contacts and stumbled upon a number that she had always saved in her phone, but never dialed: her father.

"Hello?"

"Daddy?" Jazmyn said with a small voice. Just that quickly, this man had answered the phone and made her revert all the way back to the seven year old child that she'd been before he left.

"Who is this?" He sounded angry. Jazmyn paused before speaking. She was surprised. She knew that he hadn't spoke to her in years and obviously wasn't interested in being her father, but she never expected him to be angry at her for calling.

"This is...Daddy, this is Jazmyn. Your daughter." She whispered into the phone. There was a long pause. She wasn't sure he had heard her. She opened her mouth to repeat herself, but then he spoke.

"Jazmyn." Was all he said.

"Yes, Jazmyn." Then Jazmyn heard another voice in the background. It was a young woman.

"Daddy? Are you read for dinner? We are going to go over all the details for the wedding...I can't wait for you to see my dress!" Jazmyn felt like her heart was being ripped out of her chest. A wedding. She was at the lowest point in her life and her father was preparing to walk her half-sister down the aisle so she could get married off to the man of her dreams.

"Listen...um, I'm kinda in the middle of something. So....bye." He hung up the phone before she even had a chance to respond. Just like that the faucet went dry and Jazmyn stopped crying. Everything was clear now. She knew what she had to do.

Jazmyn walked over to her dresser and opened the top drawer. In it was a brand new shiny, silver .45 caliber pistol that she had bought a couple weeks ago. She pulled it out and kissed it. She had never used this gun; her weapon of choice had always been her machete or her smaller blades. That was what Crimson had taught her to use, and it's what she felt most comfortable with also. It almost seemed like it was meant to be that she would choose this weapon, one she had never used to do something that she'd thought she'd never do.

Jazmyn walked over to her desk and pulled out some stationary that her mother had bought her when she had first passed the bar and became an attorney. It was much too flowery and frilly for her and she had been uncomfortable using it. But at this moment, she was grateful for it. She grabbed a pen and sat down on the bed with the gun beside her.

Dear Mama, I just want to let you know that I love you very much and I always will. This is not your fault, so don't ever think that. This is all my fault. You did your part as a mother...you did all that you could do. I have sinned so much in my life and I can never right my wrongs. I've hurt people who didn't deserve it and I'm afraid I can't face myself any longer. I hope that you forgive me. I hope that you can still love me. Every woman is born a Queen...some just have a longer journey to their throne. That's what you always told me. I'm sorry I gave up. I'm sorry that I never reached my throne. I'm sorry I never made you proud. I love you, mama.

I love you forever and I'm sorry,

Jazmyn

Jazmyn looked through her tear-filled eyes at the letter before kissing it and folding it together. She laid it next to her on the bed and grabbed the gun.

"Oh my God...please forgive me! Please forgive me, God. Have mercy upon my soul, I pray!" Jazmyn whispered to herself. With that, she turned off the safety and placed the gun at her temple. Then she changed her mind. She decided that she wanted to shoot the blackest and most evil part of herself, so she aimed it at her heart. And pulled the trigger.

The next part of this series, '3 Kings,' is the finale.

A GLIMPSE OF 3 KINGS

SALEM

*T*he look on their faces was priceless.

Kaylen was staring at me as if she was about to pee in her pants and Zo was gawking at me as if he owed me something. Fuck it, that nigga did owe me something. Yeah, I was on some stupid shit the last time he saw me, but there was no reason for him to try to kill my ass over a bitch.

Then I get back here and this nigga is sitting in here chilling in her house. So pretty much, while my ass was going through rehab to get my body in order *and* to get over my addiction, he was in here feeling so sorry about killing me that he'd decided to start fucking around with Kaylen. Yeah, that nigga owed me a lot. But I would get to that later.

"What are you doing here? I thought you were..." Zo started.

"What? Dead? You thought I was dead because you shot me, right? Because of her," I said jabbing my finger in Kaylen's direction. She jumped back like I was going to hit her or something. It almost made me laugh.

"What you jumping for?" I asked her. She didn't say a word; she just continued to stare at me. "I'm not going to do anything to you. You got your bodyguard here to protect you anyways, right? He can shoot me again and then you can fuck him as his consolation prize for killing his best friend….again." I wasn't expecting it, but for a second, a shadow of guilt passed over her face. But it was quickly replaced by anger.

"Salem, you getting out of line, bro. Now we can talk if you wanna talk, but…" Zo started as he walked closer to the entrance of the door.

"No, fuck that shit! You can talk to him on your own time. Get the fuck off of my property, Salem! Now!" Kaylen yelled. "You have five seconds before I get my gun and come out shooting!"

"Hey, you don't have to tell me more than once." I raised my hands into the air. "I didn't even come here to start no drama. I really just wanted to chat with you…and apologize. I'm better now, if you can't tell. That's all it was, really…then I saw my boy's car in your yard, so…"

"Leave! Now!" Kaylen said again.

I shrugged before turning around to head back to my Escalade. I jumped in and started pulling out of the yard. Before I left, I made sure to roll down the window and chuck the deuces at Zo and Kaylen while they watched me.

It really was all good. My intent was to stop by and talk to Kaylen. I wanted to apologize to her for all the shit that I had done. My mind was gone the last time she saw me. I was on some stupid shit…I had never fucked around with Meth in the past and I never would ever again. That shit had my mind blown. My next stop was to meet up with my boy. Zo had been my nigga since we were little. I hadn't faulted him once for shooting me that night. Hell, if it had been me getting jumped on by a cracked out ass nigga, I would have shot him, too. I wanted to speak to him, show him I was well, and tell him that everything was all good between us…water under the bridge.

But now that I saw what they had been up to since I'd "been murdered," I wasn't about to forgive shit.

"Man, fuck that hoe ass bitch and the bitch ass nigga. Fuckers been out here living the life, not feeling guilty for shit! I thought that nigga was my best friend, but he killed me *over* this bitch and then decided to start *fucking* with this bitch!"

I couldn't help but think about how I had been in rehab the whole time, with the only thing making me press through it being the thought that I could show back up, apologize to Kaylen, repair our relationship, and eventually marry her. I knew it would take some time to do it, but it was what I had dreamed about every night and thought about every day. I wanted her to be mine.

But I returned home for what? This shit. My very first stop after being let out of rehab was to pick up my car and drive to her house. I got there and she wasn't home, I thought she had probably moved, so I broke in so I could be sure. She hadn't moved; everything was just as it was when I had left. Except all my shit was gone. That pissed me off, so I pulled out the cufflinks that she had bought me, the ones I had been carrying around in my pocket, and I sat them on top of the dresser in one of the guestrooms. I locked Tiny up in the room to make sure she would see them and think of me.

I waited a few days and figured I would try again. I had it all thought out in my mind. My apology had been rehearsed every day that I had been in rehab going through detox and every second that I endured of physical therapy. I pushed myself through some of the hardest times thinking that it would all be fine once I got back to her. And I got here to find out that she's been fucking around with my best friend the entire time.

Payback is about to be a bitch.

NOTE FROM PORSCHA STERLING

Thank you for reading! Please join my mailing list to stay up-to-date on my next releases! Text PORSCHA to 25827 to join.

I truly do hope that you enjoyed learning about the 3 Queens. Kaylen, Alexis and Jazmyn are characters very close to my heart and they have a lot more in store for them.

You can complete this series by reading 3 Kings. You also should check out Vanessa and Ty's love story in Unstoppable Love and then the The Wife of a Hustler series.

Please make sure to leave a review! I love reading them!

I would love it if you reach out to me on Facebook, Instagram or Twitter! Search 'Porscha Sterling's VIP Readers' on Facebook to join my reading group!

Peace, love & blessings to everyone. I love allllll of you!

Porscha Sterling

ABOUT THE AUTHOR

Porscha Sterling is an African-American Romance author and publisher of Royalty Publishing House, Inc.

Join Porscha's Mailing List. Text PORSCHA to 25827
To find out more about her, visit her website

READ MORE ON THE LIT READING APP!

Read more books like this one **for less**! Check out some other new releases on the LiT Reading App. Go to www.litreadingapp.com to learn more!

www.ingramcontent.com/pod-product-compliance
Lightning Source LLC
Chambersburg PA
CBHW051300250626
47155CB00009B/3366